Pretty Monsters

T. Edward Redd

Everything in this story is fictional. I made it all up. Names, characters, and incidents are either from imagination or used in a fictitious manner. Any resemblance to actual persons, living or dead, or actual events is purely coincidental...

THANKS YOU

I want to thank my father for always pushing me to believe in myself. You've never been the type of parent to discourage a child's dream. Instead you have supported me and believed in me when I didn't believe in myself. You take interest in my dreams and passions. Thank you for never telling me I couldn't write to save my life. My greatest wish is to become a great father like you someday.

I also want to thank my mother and sister for their support. Thank you mother for coming to my first book signing. It was very motivating and I will always cherish the love you two bring to my life.

Thank you, Austin Owens for being like a brother to me. You're really inspiring and you encourage me to perfect my crafts as you perfect your own. I can see great things coming your way. Thanks goes out to the *rest of the Owens family for supporting me as well. Thank you, Mark and Austin for coming to my first book signing.*

Special thanks goes to Betty Lorentz for telling me the plot to one of my upcoming novels was good and also for reading Hero's Romance. It inspired me to write more and set publishing goals. If it wasn't for that I don't think Pretty Monsters would have gotten ready for publication. I really hope you enjoy the book I told you about. I wish you the best luck towards your college ventures and dreams.

Thank you Keila Blue Butterfly Dragon for inspiring me to specifically publish Pretty Monsters. This book is a four-year project and I cherish it dearly. Thank you for encouraging me to finally put it out.

Tylor Smith you rock. Thank you for being a good example of the type of person I want to be as far as success goes. It's very inspiring to watch you progress with your films. I hope to see you do great things.

Thank you Ariya Marr for proofreading my very first book and helping me perfect it. I don't think I put you on the acknowledgement page in Hero's Romance. But you deserve a thank you. If you happen to read this book, I hope you enjoy it.

Thank you Jonathon Williams for constantly asking to read manuscripts for my stories. It's really motivating. Especially when I'm being lazy and not writing or coming up with story ideas. You've been reading my stories since before I finished my first book. You are awesome and I thank you. Keep chasing your dreams. I support you.

Thank you to everyone who takes the time to read this book. It means a lot to me.

Last but not least thank you, Sammi. Without you Samantha Black's character would have never been inspired. I haven't seen you since high school and have no idea where you are or how you're doing. But if you happen to read this book one day, I hope that you remember it and how it came to be. You. Thank you for inspiring my very first and most treasured book character. I hope you're doing well.

CONTENTS

1. *Fade into Black*

I usually took the time to comb my hair in the mornings. I hated leaving home with wild hair. But that morning I didn't care. All I wanted to do was go back to bed, bury myself in the sheets and try to forget. But I couldn't. I had to face school eventually. I had already missed too many days. It was senior year and I couldn't throw away three years of hardwork. I needed to work had to catch up.

I put on the first thing I could find. I put on blue jeans and a burgundy wool sweater. My hair was still a mess. I just wanted the day that had barely started to end. After a lot of reluctant effort I forced myself out of my quiet home. It was hard to ignore the cruel winds of the fall weather.

I looked at the sky as I shut the door behind me. The sun was shining bright and the skies were painted with different soft shades of blue. There were a few clouds here and there. It kind of made me smile. Was it a sign of a good day? No. Suddenly a few clouds blocked off the sunlight. Then I remembered everything that made me stay home for so long.

Pain.

I got into my ten year old, silver car and the drive to school began. Why couldn't I just stay home a little longer? How could I face it? Things would be so weird and painful. I just wanted to rewind time back to the summer before. Maybe I could have said something to change her mind. The more I thought of it, the more I wanted to hold her warm and soft hand. I still couldn't understand what happened.

After the long and quiet drive, I was at my high school. It was nothing out of the ordinary. It had space for a couple thousands of students. The inside had softly painted royal blue walls, white tiles and long and quiet hallways filled with lockers. When I passed the lounge area I got a strong whiff of coffee. It was just a typical high school. The only thing out of the ordinary about it was Caroline Green.

The more I thought about her the more depressed and pitiful I felt. I pushed her to the furthest part of my mind and walked to my third period class. When I walked inside everyone stopped what they were doing.

The boy who vanished for months had returned. Professor Grays was writing on the board in front of the class. When he stopped to ask a question, he saw me. He stared, cleaned his glasses and crinkled his bushy mustache. It was like he couldn't believe I came.

"Thomas," he said in an overly surprised tone. "You've shown up for class? It ends in about fifteen minutes but I'm still glad to see you. The teachers were worried. Are you ok?"

He handed me an assignment packet. I didn't give a verbal response. Just a shrug and a grunt. I ignored the dozens of eyes watching me. I walked to the middle of the classroom and took my seat. I could feel them all staring at me. Trying to invade my mind. No words were spoken but I could hear all of the thoughts.

"What happened?"

"Why did you two break up?"

"Will you get back together?"

I hid away in the world of history, letting hundreds of the book's pages hide my face.

"Thomas!" I heard someone whisper.

I looked back. It was my friend, Ace. His actual name was Albert. He was a sort of round kid with short hair, brown skin and glasses. He usually wore sweatpants with some sort of anime t-shirt.

I watched as he sketched Japanese cartoons in his pad. Typical Ace. His thick brown fingers held the pencil delicately as the lead paced back and forth, then in circles on the paper. I never understood how people could be so talented with just a sheet of paper and pencil. He looked and realized I was watching him.

He whispered, "Oh. I didn't think you heard me. Where've you been? School started in August and it's almost September."

"I know that," I said, trying not to be heard.

He said, "Is this about Caroline? It's been almost three months. Dude you..."

"Stop," I interrupted.

He took in a deep breath, nodded and started drawing again. Being so harsh felt bad but so was my mood. He was going to say, move on. Everyone did. They said it as if it were the easiest thing to do. Caroline was, perfect and my best friend. I turned away from him and hid again.

It upset me that he would even think to say that. Everyone knew how much she meant to me. Yet they just kept telling me to forget and let go. Move on. It's not like I could turn my feelings on and off like some faucet. I hated how they all thought it was that easy.

Then I heard laughter. That *really* got to me. I quickly turned back, trying to figure out who it was. But they weren't laughing at *me*. It was a girl I had never seen before. I nearly forgot why I was upset. She made me so...speechless.

She had hints of blush on her face and her skin was radiant. Her hair stuck out the most. It was red like roses and wavy, reaching her back. She wore this black sundress. It was decorated with white floral designs over the black fabric. She was reading some classic novel. Not a care in the world.

As she flipped a page I saw her smile ever so slightly. I started to smile with her. But the moment was ruined when a tiny paper wad hit her in the face. Her smile slowly turned into this blank stare.

Her eyes shut. I just knew she was going to cry or yell at them. Or so I thought. She opened her eyes and kept reading, never flinching or anything. The boys kept snickering and tossing things at her. But it was like she couldn't see or hear them. She was unbelievably calm.

The kids at my school were always like that. They could be really annoying and cruel. Especially to the new kids. I didn't understand why it was like that. All she was doing was reading. And I'm sure she hated the school. Who would blame her?

Without any warning she moved her eyes in my direction. She never moved her head, neck or body. Just her eyes. Had the teacher called on her? I looked back but he was writing on the board as he spoke to the class. I looked back at her. Her eyes were still locked on me. I couldn't look away. I tried to figure out what she was saying with her eyes. She never smiled, frowned or even blinked. Why was her stare so familiar yet unknown?

The lunch bell rung and it made me flinch. I jumped in my seat and shut my eyes. Everyone rushed out of their seats like there was a fire. I tried catching sight of the girl but the crowds of students blocked my vision. When the space was cleared her seat was empty. I didn't blame her. I'd race out too if the kids were harassing me like that.

After I got my things, I left the class. Ace followed. The halls were moderately filled with kids. There was enough people to make my ears ring but not enough to keep me from walking. I focused on the lunchroom. It was a couple of yards away. Caroline's third period was close to mine. I knew she would be close and I didn't want to see her.

Ace was talking nonstop. With the loud voices, footsteps of students and my spacing out, I hadn't heard a word he said. He got impatient and grabbed me.

He said, "Thomas! Did you hear me? The new episode of *Monster Fighter* came on last night. It was awesome! Louis saved Abby! Can you believe she's an actual pixie? Thomas? Thomas!"

"I hear you!" I said. "Ace I have a lot on my mind ok? I didn't watch the stupid cartoon last night. I slept all day."

He said, "So you've been home sleeping. The guys were right."

I ignored him. The café was feet away and I

managed not to see Caroline.

He continued, "You have to get over her! It's been three months."

That's when I almost lost it. But then I heard laughter. It made me forget about Ace and made me panic. My eyes made their way to a group of girls just a few feet away. Veronica and Emily.

Veronica was Caroline's best friend. They were practically inseparable. Where Caroline went, Veronica went. Unless of course, Caroline had a date with me. Then Veronica had to stay home and sulk. She sometimes tried to be the third wheel but it hardly ever worked once Caroline and I got serious.

Emily was another one of Caroline's friends. But she wasn't as close as Veronica. Most of Caroline's friends were the next to be *Veronica*. The next best friend if Veronica and Caroline ever got into a fight or something. It never happened though. Caroline and Veronica never fought about anything.

I watched Veronica talk to Emily. She was twirling her long and brown hair like she always did. She had it just like Caroline's. Except Caroline's hair was jet black with bangs. Natural. No dye. No one believed her but me. The only reason I knew was because I grew up with her. Caroline and I had been friends for a pretty long time before we got together.

I knew Caroline had to be nearby if Veronica was standing there against the lockers. I couldn't help but watch and search. Ace pulled my arm.

He said, "Hey. Come on, let's keep walking. Ignore them."

But it was too late. Veronica noticed me. She shot me a smile and leaned over to her left. Caroline came from the sea of students. She looked surprised to see me. Then guilty. Why? Did she regret the breakup?

She had been acting so strange since summer. I couldn't figure her out. She just stood there gawking at me. When I raised my hand to wave, she shook her head no and turned away. Veronica and Emily started laughing hysterically.

I stormed off towards the café. Ace had to do a little jog to catch up, almost dropping his things. Everything seemed to get louder when I walked into the lunchroom. There was so much noise and talking. All I wanted was quiet and time to myself. I wasn't ready to be back. Everything and everyone was starting to annoy me.

Ace noticed. He said, "It's going to be alright. Just relax and breathe. Let's go see the guys. We can just sit and relax."

I shook my head. He didn't deserve any backlash from my bad mood. He meant well and was trying to help. So I followed him to our usual lunch table.

As they normally did, the rest of my friends were sitting at the round table. Martinez, Williams and Tylor.

Martinez was a mixed kid with curly brown hair. He usually wore jeans and some button up shirt. He was the group's jokester. He was usually the one to get us laughing.

Tylor was what I guess you could call our group leader. He did all of the get-togethers and we mostly hung out at his house. He was a tall, pale and skinny kid with short brown hair.

Williams was my closest friend out of the four. He was tall, lean and dark skinned. He was a bookworm. He was always reading some history book. He even wore these thin black glasses. I had known him since before Caroline switched schools. He was pretty quiet for the most part unless you get him excited. I'm pretty sure he was the smartest out of all of us.

For the most part we all always hung out with eachother. But I had been gone for a few months. So they were pretty excited to see me.

Martinez was overly excited. "Hey! Thomas is back," he said.

They all watched Ace and I sit. Even Tylor was watching. Normally he was too busy writing stories to notice much. So when he wasn't writing you knew something was up.

Ace said, "He's still bummed about the breakup."

Why he said that, I don't know. But it annoyed me even more. She was the last thing I wanted to talk about. But it was an inevitable topic. High school love gossip.

Martinez said my most hated phrase. "You have to get over her, man. Besides, Veronica is having a pool soon. There will be plenty of girls there."

I ignored that comment. Veronica was Caroline's best friend. I wasn't going to go to any party where she was going to be. As I started eating my food, I heard laughter again. It was just like the laughter in the classroom. I looked behind me. Sure enough, it was the same girl being made fun of again. She was sitting alone and reading, while a group of kids laughed and pointed at her.

"Hey you guys," I said.

Martinez leaned in saying, "His first words. Guys, he's talking!"

I was too distracted to sass him back. I said, "Who's that girl with the pretty red hair? The one sitting at that table by herself."

Tylor sighed as he shook his head. "Oh gosh. No, Thomas. Leave that one alone."

Martinez said, "She transferred here last week. She's new but I would listen to Tylor. Trust me."

She was just reading. Yet I couldn't stop looking at her. She was so gorgeous and seemed peaceful. Seeing her made me happy that I was back at school. Who was she?

Tylor said, "Seriously, man. Don't."

"Huh?" I said. "I'm just wondering why she's sitting alone."

Ace said, "You haven't been here, so you don't know. But she's creepy and weird. Weirder than Isabella Butler."

"Yeah right," I scoffed. "No one's weirder than Isabella."

All at once they pointed at the red head. I quickly got up and put their hands down. I said, "Cut that out! She'll see us and feel like an outcaste."

"She is!" said Tylor. "She's really quiet. I don't think I've ever heard her talk. She only talks to teachers. No one will sit by her in classes."

I sat down saying, "I wonder if it has something to do with harassment. I've been here less than an hour and I've seen her get picked on twice. All she's doing is reading." I looked at her again.

Ace said, "Dude! It's because she's weird. You haven't been here long enough to know."

"How much can you learn about a person in a week?" I said. "I bet no one has even welcomed her here. She dresses differently, but big deal. I feel bad for her. She probably hates it here."

I started eating my food again. Then they started whispering to eachother and laughing. I slammed my fork down and said, "What?"

Martinez said, "You're in love with the creepy girl."

Everyone but Williams started laughing. I didn't take it to heart. That's how we usually joked around. But something about that moment started bugging me. I stayed home for so long. I went back to school hoping things had changed. But everyone and everything was the same. I started wishing I had stayed home. Everything and everyone was annoying me. Except one person.

She was still sitting there reading, while the kids laughed at her. Why wasn't she reacting to the them? Why was I so attracted to her? I should have been thinking about Caroline. But something about that new girl made me forget about *everything*. She was so new and unknown. At that moment it was a good thing. She was the only thing at the school that didn't depress me.

Before I knew it, I was walking towards her. My friends kept trying to convince me not to go. But my feet kept dragging me until I was at her table. The room seemed to get more and more quiet as I got close. As I sat down she watched me from the corner of her eyes. It was in the same manner as she did in class. Nothing moved but her eyes. I thought she might not have wanted me there.

Casually I shrugged and said, "What? It's the lunchroom. I can sit wherever I want right?" I could feel her eyes still locked on me when I started eating again. She shut her eyes. When they opened, their focus was on the novel in her hands. The silence was making me feel weird. So she really *was* quiet.

"So you're new?" I said. Her eyes shifted toward me again. They were just eyes. But the way she looked at me was like nothing I had ever experienced before.

Her deep brown eyes spoke this serene and mysterious silence. I wanted to know what they were trying to say so badly. What was this familiarity mixed with unknown that I was feeling? It didn't bother me at all. I was glad she hadn't told me to get lost. I smiled and turned to my food.

I said, "Well I hope you like it here. Welcome to Blue Lake Central."

"Thank you, Thomas," she said.

We had never spoken before. So when she said my name it surprised me. I asked her how she knew it. She had this incredibly exotic accent. If I had to guess where she was from I would have said Europe.

She said, "Thomas is the name our teacher used when you arrived today. What's your surname?"

"My what?"

She smiled softly as her eyes went back to her book. She had a very calm attitude. She did everything slowly but not too slowly. Now that I was close I could tell she wasn't upset at all. She was just very peaceful and quiet, like a river. The longer I sat there the more drawn I got to her.

She said, "Your full name. What is your full name?" Her eyes were still on the book.

"Oh," I said quickly. "It's Thomas Rouges. How about you? What's your name?"

She spoke casually, "Samantha…" she turned a page, "…Black."

I don't know why but this girl was blowing me away. All she was doing was reading. I couldn't wrap my mind around why I was so drawn to her.

"Wow," I said. "That's a cool name. Samantha Black. It's catchy. Samantha are you from here?"

My smile faded as she turned her body to me for the first time. She was so serene and soft. Yet her presence was really heavy. She was beautiful but in a way that commanded attention, never demanding it.

Her long hair was resting on her shoulders. I couldn't get over how well the black dress went so well against her skin. Then our eyes met again. Samantha was watching me. But she hadn't said a word. It was like she was trying to invade my mind. It felt like she was looking inside of then right through me. Her stare was impossible to word.

I said, "Samantha. Why are you looking at me like that?"

"So then, you aren't here to poke fun of or taunt me." She said it like it was a fact, not a question.

"Of course not," I said. "Those guys were real jerks. You were really mature about it though. Sorry you have to deal with that. It's nothing personal. They haze all of the new kids. I should know…"

I had to stop myself. I realized I was hazed like Samantha up until Caroline arrived. No one bugged me because of how popular she became. Suddenly the mood felt cold and murky. I was reminded that Caroline was no longer with me. It felt like it was raining. But when Samantha spoke the rain stopped.

She said, "You're kind. Thank you." Her eyes were on me again. She was giving me her full attention. I scoot close and leaned in to look at the novel.

I said, "Don't worry about it. It's the right thing to do. So what book is this? I feel like I've seen it before."

"*Hero's Wake,*" she said.

I got closer to read a few lines. Then I felt something lie on my shoulder. It was her hair. Samantha's face was *really* close to mine and she was getting closer. I got this hot rush all over me. I wanted to kiss her. I wanted to grab her hips and meet her lips with mine. I had never felt so eager and nervous at one time.

On impulse I dumbly blurted, "What are you doing?"

She gasped and flinched away as if she snapped out of some daydream. She apologized, quickly got up and started walking away fast. I barely had time to chase after her.

"Samantha wait up," I said.

I reached for her hand. She pulled it away and swatted me into a seat. When I gained my senses she was walking out of the café. I got up as fast as I could and paced after her. Then I noticed the room was still really quiet. Too quiet. That's when I realized that they had all been watching us. Some were whispering to one another. Samantha pulled so much of my attention that I hadn't noticed. I ignored them and left the café. But she was gone.

"Very smooth, Casanova," I heard a familiar voice say. My skin nearly ran off of my body as I turned around. Isabella Butler was leaning against the café door while holding her signature black book. She carried it wherever she went.

Isabella Butler was a girl who had been obsessed with me since the eighth grade. She dropped her books one day. I helped her and she'd been after me ever since. She was pretty sure enough. Nice almond skin, long and wavy blonde hair. Her eyes were soft and dark blue. She always wore some sort of long dress. Today she was wearing a dark blue sundress. Heck I might have gone for a girl like Isabella if she wasn't so obsessive.

"Not now Isabella," I said.

She smiled and flipped her hair. She stood up straight, still holding her book to her chest as she walked towards me.

She said, "I was wondering when you'd come back. You know it gets pretty boring here when you're gone." She was next to me. She said, "So Miss Green broke your heart. Hate to say I told you so. That girl is nothing but trouble. More than you know."

I kept walking as I scoffed. "Isabella, please. I don't want to talk about her ok?"

She said, "All I'm saying is that I did warn you. Did I not? I told you she would hurt you. Do you want me to do something about it? Just say the word." I noticed her staring at her black book. Her fingers were rubbing along the closed pages.

She said, "Should I talk to Miss Green?"

"No. Don't say anything to her," I said. "What's the deal with that thing. You never put it down."

She looked at me and smiled. "My diary. I wouldn't want anyone to see the things I write in here." She got closer. "Anyone except you that is. The things I write in here would make you warm all over. Want to read it?"

I shook my head and nudged her off of my shoulder. "No thank you. Just don't say or do anything to Caroline. Her friends would seriously hurt you."

She nodded. "Fine, my love. If you change your mind, let me know. So are you getting back with Miss Green anytime before tomorrow?"

I shook my head no.

She got close again. She said softly, "Why don't you let me help you forget about her. Let me take you out or something. Maybe a nice movie or dine out."

I said, "Isabella I don't feel like going out tonight. I'm just going to go home and sleep."

"Hm. Do you want company while you sleep?" She touched my hand.

I pulled away and said, "Isabella I just got back today! Seriously, you're being more pushy than usual. Can you go study in the library or something?"

"No. I can't help it. I've waited forever for the day that you two came apart. Now it's here and I won't let you slip through my fingers again. Miss Green blew her chance and *Miss Black* won't get one."

I stopped walking to look at her. She was smirking.

"You know Samantha?" I asked.

"I saw you two together in there. She got pretty close to your face." She placed her book in one hand and the other around my waist. She pulled me close saying, "Only I will be getting this close to you."

I pushed her away. "Isabella seriously! Knock it off. How do you know Samantha?"

She smiled and looked away. "I know a lot about a lot. I'll tell you everything in exchange for a date."

"Pass," I said as I walked past her.

She persisted as usual. She said, "Fine. Can I at least walk you to class, my love?"

I shook my head yes because saying no to Isabella was always pointless. She followed me even when I said no. Caroline was the only person who could keep her away. Isabella never did anything life threatening or serious. The teachers never took my complaints serious. She was just a high school girl with a crush. Unfortunately that crush was me.

She walked with me to science class. She talked senselessly the entire time. But I couldn't stop thinking about Samantha. I felt bad. I might have embarrassed her in front of everyone. I didn't want to become another person who made her life Hell at school. It's not like I didn't want to kiss her. It just caught me by surprise.

I sat in class thinking about her. She hadn't

returned from lunch. So I figured she had a different fourth period class. But after class she never showed up in any of my other classes. My last period class, art, seemed to drag for the last hour.

"What the hell, Thomas!" I heard someone whisper. I looked back to see Tylor. He said, "You're with the new girl now? Have you lost your mind? Why, Thomas? I told you she was weird!"

"With her?" I said. "I'm not with her and she isn't weird. She's actually pretty nice. Anyway, I'm pretty sure I'll never see her again anyway."

He whispered loudly, "What are you talking about? Everyone saw you two making out in the café."

"Making out?"

"Yes," he said. He was barely keeping quiet. "The whole school saw, including your ex. You know, the one you're still in love with?" I looked back to see him pointing at Caroline. She and her friends quickly turned away.

I turned to him saying, "We were only talking. We never kissed."

"That's not what the entire school thinks," he said.

I turned away but not before noticing the other students watching me discreetly. After classes ended, I searched for Samantha. But she was nowhere to be found. Who was this girl?

I found myself in the office contemplating on asking about her. But it felt so creepy and weird. I had just met her and now I was trying to get personal information on her.

"Stalking, Miss Black, my love?"

I looked back to see Isabella. She was smiling and batting her eyes. She walked towards me. She said, "You won't find her now. She leaves as soon as the bell rings at 2:50. She doesn't even go to her locker. Actually I've never seen her use one."

"Not now, Isabella. I'm in the middle of something."

She held up a piece of paper. "But I thought you wanted to know about Miss Black."

"What's that?"

She winked. "Her information. Address, phone number, birth date, favorite color, zodiac sign. Lots more. Want it?"

She walked to me and placed it in my hand. I took the piece of paper in my hand but she didn't let go. She said, "Miss Black won't let you get near her. Trust me. She's going to blow you off. When she does you're going to take me out. Deal?"

"Blow me off? How do you know that?"

She smiled. "I know more things than you can imagine, my love. Take this piece of paper and go chase that redheaded damsel. But when she turns you away, come see me. Deal?"

"Fine," I said as I took the paper.

She smiled wide and clapped her hands. "Marvelous! Oh gosh. I can't wait to hold your hand. I promise not to hurt you like Miss Green did. I swear it, my love."

As she talked, Tylor and Williams ran into the office. Williams said, "There you are!"

Tylor said, "Caroline and her friends are about to beat up the new girl! Caroline is pissed at her for kissing you!"

"Thomas did *not* kiss that hideous creature," Isabella barked. She said, "They were just talking."

Tylor came over and took my hand (thankfully). He said, "Yeah whatever. You can stalk him later Isabella." They lead me out of the office.

When we went outside I couldn't believe my eyes. Crowds of students were gathered in front of the school parking lot. In the center was Emily, another one of Caroline's friends Chloe, Veronica and of course Caroline. They were standing in front of Samantha.

Caroline always had the habit of chasing off girls who had any sort of interest in me. Especially when we were little. But this took the cake. I pushed through the crowds and got close enough to hear them taunting her.

Caroline glared at Samantha and said, "You have a lot of nerve. You haven't been here but a week and you're all over him."

Chloe added, "You probably don't know. But Thomas is Caroline's. So you better watch yourself."

Caroline said, "Exactly. Obviously he feels sorry for you. Don't start thinking he actually likes you."

Samantha just stood there. She was looking towards them but wasn't focusing on anyone. If I didn't know any better I'd say she was staring off into space or just ignoring them. Her book was still in her hand. Even though the moment was chaotic I was happy to see her again.

Veronica said, "Do you think you can just come here and start kissing random boys?"

Caroline laughed cruelly as she said, "Are you even going to talk? Or are you scared?"

Samantha calmly said, "I will only tell you one time. Step out of my way and leave me alone."

The girls started laughing. I started to worry for Samantha's safety. She was new and clearly didn't know how cruel the girls could get.

Caroline said, "The poor baby wants us to leave her alone? Ok we will. After we teach you a lesson." The crowds started egging her on as they wooed in low voices. Chloe saw me and told Caroline I was watching. She saw me and smiled.

Caroline said to me, "So is this your new girlfriend? She's a bit of a downgrade don't you think?"

I said, "Caroline she didn't do anything wrong. All we did was talk. Leave her alone right now."

"Oh please!" Veronica barked. "Everyone saw you two sharing tongues."

Before I could say anything, Caroline said, "Pick Thomas. If you had to pick one of us, who would it be?"

At first I was confused. Then it hit me that Caroline wanted me back or something along those lines. She was making me pick between her and Samantha Black. I didn't know how I felt about it. I watched as Samantha stared off into space. It's as if she couldn't see anyone or anything around her. What was it about her that spoke so loud yet quietly?

"Hey!" Caroline shouted. " Didn't you hear me? Which is it? Me or her?"

I said, "Caroline I don't get you. You haven't been yourself since last summer. I don't want to do this right here in front of all of these people. Regardless, you need to leave Samantha alone. Stop this right now and tell your friends to back off."

That's when the crowds started laughing and adding to the chaos. I didn't think before I spoke. I was just defending Samantha. She was severely outmatched and everyone treated her differently. I didn't want to be like them. She didn't deserve to be tormented. As I told Caroline to stop, Samantha finally focused. Her eyes were on me and she looked surprised. Was she expecting me to take Caroline's side?

Caroline got more irritated. She said, "Are you serious? Just say me! You're choosing this loner over me? Ugh!" She took a moment to breathe, then she was smirking confidently again. She said, "Fine. But let's see how you like her when her face is all scratched up. Girls!" On cue her friends gathered around Samantha.

I gasped. "Hey! Caroline don't!" The crowd held me back as her friends started their assault. Chloe was the first to go in. She swung her hand at Samantha but thankfully missed. Then she swung again. Still she missed.

Emily laughed. "Knock it off! Get that freak."

Chloe just stood there for a moment.

She said, "Did you girls see her move?" I watched her stare at Samantha. Chloe looked confused then nervous. Slowly she backed away and bumped into Caroline. She looked back with shock.

Caroline laughed. "You have got to be kidding me. You're scared of that loner?"

"Huh? Of course not!" She said. "It's just she messed with *your* guy. You should be the one to put that freak in her place. Right girls?"

Veronica laughed. "What a chicken. I'll deal with her then. Move."

Caroline got in front of them and said, "No. Chloe's right. I'll deal with…" She stopped talking when she finally noticed Samantha had moved. The girls looked everywhere but where she went. She was right behind them. I have no idea how she moved so fast.

Caroline looked over her shoulder and jumped a little. She said, "Agh! How'd you get back there?"

Samantha never spoke a word. When I told Caroline to stop again, she got even more upset. She ran at Samantha and swung her hand at her. Everyone gasped and got quiet when Samantha rose her hand as well.

She caught Caroline's wrist. All I could hear was Samantha's book hitting the ground. She wasn't staring off into space or at me. She was looking right at Caroline. They were face to face.

Caroline shouted. "Hey! Let got!"

I heard Samantha say soft yet firmly, "I warned you."

She squeezed Caroline's wrist. I watched her try to break Samantha's grip repeatedly but it was useless. Samantha never moved at all. She just stood there holding Caroline's wrist and watching her.

Caroline suddenly stopped and said, "You better let go. Or you'll be sorry! You don't have a clue who you're messing with."

Samantha didn't say anything back. Suddenly

Caroline was trying to pull away as if death was holding her. It was so random but she was freaking out.

"Let go! LET ME GO!"

Caroline pulled and jerked away. Samantha's body never moved. It was like Caroline's hand was trapped under a rock. She fell down trying to pull away. Samantha just stood there as she watched Caroline. I couldn't figure out why she was freaking out so badly.

Caroline shouted, "Let go! Help! Get her OFF!" It was like some vicious animal was attacking her. Everyone started laughing as her friends went in to help.

"Let her go you freak!" Veronica said.

It seemed like the word *freak* got Samantha's attention. As soon as Veronica said it, Samantha let go and turned to her. Caroline didn't hesitate to break away and crawl far away from Samantha. She was breathing so fast it was like she just escaped a chokehold. The rest of the girls went to her. Samantha stood there, still very calm and quiet.

Veronica said, "Caroline get a grip! All she did was hold your hand!"

She stood up quickly and screamed. I assumed from anger and embarrassment. She said, "You are so dead!" She stopped when, Samantha started walking towards her.

Caroline stood her ground saying, "Freak. I am warning you. Don't get any closer!"

Samantha ignored her. She got a few feet away and stopped.

"Don't you dare," Caroline hissed.

Samantha smiled lightly and bent down. Her book was lying in front of Caroline. She picked it up and wiped dirt off of it. She turned away and started walking away as if nothing had ever happened.

The crowds of students parted into an aisle for her. Right before she was out of it, she stopped and looked back. It was me who she looked at briefly. It felt like days but it was only a few seconds. Then she walked away. My fingers rubbed against the paper still balled inside of my hand. I held it up and opened it. Isabella went above and beyond for me.

2. On the Hill

I couldn't figure out what happened with Caroline. What did Samantha do that made her freak out so badly? All she did was grab Caroline's wrist. To be fair, Caroline was the one who threw her hand first. She would have slapped Samantha across the face. So why did it scare her so badly when Samantha defended herself?

A whole week had went by since I saw Samantha. I started to think she transferred out. Why wouldn't she? Everyone besides me singled her out to be made fun of. She was the school outcaste. I couldn't understand why. When I spoke to her she came off as polite and pleasant. There was nothing weird about her.

When I thought about her I would sometimes touch my cheek. She came so close that day. Her lips almost touched my face. I had to go and ruin the moment by embarrassing her. Why couldn't I get her out of my mind? Samantha Black had penetrated a spot inside of me only Caroline had managed to get to.

It had only been two months since the break-up.

Just the other week I'd give anything to be with her again. But now there was this new girl who had so discreetly became the person I thought about the most. All it took was a glance at her deep brown eyes.

Even my friends began to notice I was acting different. I would stare off into space more and more. Thinking about Samantha. I still had the piece of paper from Isabella. How did she even get it? And why was she so sure Samantha would reject me?

On a Tuesday at Tylor's house, my friends and I got together. We were all sitting in his large and wooden living room, watching tv. His house was pretty big. Enough for ten or eight people I suppose. Everyday after school we went to Tylor's to watch horror movies or play first-person shooters on his big screen. He usually made us a snack whenever Ace asked for something to eat.

That day he was going to make us sandwiches. He came out of the kitchen and said, "I'm all out of bread. Sorry, guys."

They all moaned and groaned. Except me. I was too busy looking at Samantha's address in my hand. I kept thinking about going to see her. Then I would tell myself no. It would be weird and creepy.

I hated how Isabella always followed me and basically stalked me. I wouldn't want Samantha to see me as a stalker. I wasn't going to take advice from a girl who knew nothing about boundaries.

As my friends complained about the food shortage, Tylor suggested we all go out for pizza. Everyone was with the idea. Especially, Ace.

On cue he jumped up. He said, "Yeah! As long as we get sausage and pepperoni." Second to gaming and drawing, food was his first love.

I hadn't said a word. Martinez said, "Yo! Man. Do you want pizza for dinner?"

I balled the paper up into my hand quickly. "Oh. Yeah, sure," I said.

Tylor noticed and got closer. He said, "What's that you were looking at?"

"Yeah you've been staring at it forever," Martinez said.

"Nothing. Let's go get the pizza." They clearly didn't like Samantha and I didn't want to answer any questions. I didn't even know if I was actually going to see her again.

"Guys," Ace said. "Isn't it obvious? He's clearly still hurting from the breakup."

I actually hadn't thought about that since last Wednesday. I should have been worried about Caroline but I was more worried about Samantha. I hadn't even talked to Caroline.

Tylor said, " You must be worried about her. That new girl almost killed her. I've never seen anyone scream like that before."

Martinez said, "I bet the freak got expelled. Good riddance." He sounded really disgusted.

That was one thing that never crossed my mind. Samantha expelled? Was that even possible? The idea was crazy. Samantha only defended herself. Caroline would have slapped her dead across the face. I couldn't understand why everyone was out to get her but me.

Tylor said, "Hey. What do you think, Thomas?"

I spoke without thinking. "I think everyone should get off Samantha Black's case."

Martinez said, "Whoa, easy. Wait how do you know her name?"

Tylor joined in. He got excited and said, "That's right! Those two kissed last week. Everyone saw it. So do you like her now? Is that why you skip lunch now?"

"Tell me you didn't," Martinez said. "I know the breakup was bad. But the new girl isn't exactly a good substitute. She's so…weird."

I turned to them and said, "Stop calling her stuff like that. Her name is Samantha Black. She isn't weird and we didn't kiss. I just think it sucks that everyone thinks she's some freak. She isn't."

They all just laughed as if I was telling a joke. I felt more and more sorry for her. Did the students openly laugh at her like that at school? Did she deal with it all by herself or did she have friends? Suddenly I pictured her walking home and alone in the rain, crying. What if she got depressed or something?

Martinez said, "Dude, what about Caroline? She's been with you since freshmen year. This Samantha girl just showed up two weeks ago."

Tylor agreed, "Exactly. So just leave the weird introvert alone. I'm sure there's something wrong with her."

I wanted to defend Samantha, but part of me agreed. Caroline meant a lot to me and maybe we needed to talk about things. She clearly didn't like the idea of me being with Samantha.

I stood up and said, "Let's go get the pizza. No more girl talk. My head needs a break."

We left the house while the sun was still out. I was the only person who had a car, but over the summers we walked a lot. We would talk about anything and everything and goofed around. It had become another way for us to pass time. So we were used to walking. Plus the pizzeria was only a few blocks away.

We lived in the nicer part of town. All of us were comfortable enough to eat at the pizza place even thought the sun was nearly down. Ace was the first to walk inside. It was a small building. There was white tiled flooring towards the counter where the registers were. We could always see the cooks towards the back. It was a pretty cozy spot to spend time with my friends. Most kids from our school went there after school.

It wasn't too busy so Ace was lucky enough to order fast. We all laughed to eachother when he struggled to pick toppings. Then I almost fainted.

"Thomas! Oh my gosh you've made my night!" Isabella Butler was waving from behind the counter. Unfortunately she worked at the pizzeria. Most of the time we dodged her. Sometimes we didn't.

Martinez muttered, "Oh great. She's here."

"Let's just leave," Tylor said.

But it was too late. Isabella was going over the menu and explaining all of the mouthwatering toppings. There was no way Ace would let us leave.

She said, "And today's special is pineapple with bacon and mozzarella. We have a two large for ten dollars special tonight as well." She looked at me. "But don't worry. You eat for free, my love."

"Gee thanks," I said.

"Come on. Let's go find a seat," Martinez said.

"I'll make something delicious for you, my love," Isabella said. "I'll put extra love and care into it."

We went to find a table in the dining room. After fifteen minutes, Isabella came out with our pizza. The guys got pepperoni. Ace got the special and I got my own large pizza. She made my favorite, pineapple and sausage.

Tylor said, "Hey how come he gets his for free? We're his friends. We should at least get a discount."

"I don't care about you four. You're idiots and I honestly don't know why he hangs out with you. Honey, try your pizza and make sure it's warm enough. I hand tossed it myself."

"It's fine, Isabella. Thanks."

Her face blushed as she smiled. She shook her head yes and walked back to the counter. My friends started complaining about how she called them idiots. I just sat there staring at my food. How silly did I have to be to wonder if Samantha liked pizza? I couldn't stop thinking about her. I was barely there with my friends. Mostly I was in my mind, wondering about Samantha Black.

Williams laughed, "Did you guys hear what happened to Ted Smiths?

"Yeah, didn't he go on that date with Karen Gomez," Ace said. "She's so hot. He's so lucky."

Williams went on, "After his date some guy jumped in his car while he was stopped at a stop sign. Nothing bad happen but Ted pooped himself because he was so scared. He says that's why the guy left!"

They all laughed. Tylor said, "Ted always has the coolest stories. He'll probably become a writer some day. Hey, Thomas don't you take Ap chemistry with

Ted Smiths? Thomas?"

I quickly looked up and said, "Oh yeah. That was a funny story. Karen pooped herself because Ted scared her?"

"What?" Martinez laughed. "No, man. You missed the whole story. Some guy got in his car after the date and literally scared the crap out of him." They all laughed. It was so loud the people in the front started staring at us.

"It is pretty funny," I said as I bit into my pizza.

Williams said, "Eh, he's not in a playful mood tonight."

Martinez laughed, "Yeah, he's too busy thinking about the goth girl with red hair." I ignored him until he said, "You guys have any good emo jokes?"

Ace said, "I have one. Why did the emo cross the road?" They waited. "To get a box of tissue."

They laughed a little. But it was obviously dry.

I said, "Samantha isn't emo. She's quiet and nice. She doesn't even wear makeup or eyeliner."

Martinez said, "I thought the emo crossed the road to get hit by a car."

That got to me. "Hey! That isn't funny," I shouted. They looked at me as I stood up.

Martinez waved, "Relax, man. They're jokes."

I said, "Would you guys stop it already? You guys are sitting here making fun of someone you don't even know. What if she's sitting home alone, crying because people like you can't keep their mouth shut?"

Ace dumbly said, "Dude, what if she's home right now cutting because people make fun of her?" That would explain why she isn't here. She might have committed suicide!"

My heart dropped at the thought of it. Samantha...dead? The last time anyone saw her, four girls ganged up on her. What if she couldn't handle the stress? She didn't have anyone. I started digging in my pocket for her address. I couldn't stop worrying. She didn't seem like the type to hurt herself but who knew?

"Is something wrong, my love?"

"Isabella?" I said. She had gotten beside me while I wasn't paying attention. She looked at my friends. She said, "Are these idiots bothering you? Do you want me to make them stop?"

"Oh shut it you stalker," Martinez barked. "Besides. What the hell can you do to us anyway small fry?"

She said, "More than you know, idiot."

Martinez stood up and got angry. Tylor grabbed his arm. "Stop. He doesn't like it when we talk about the Samantha girl. Just stop."

Isabella turned to me. She said, "This is about her?"

For a stalker, she was pretty open about

Samantha. I scratched my head. I said, "Well kind of. I mean…"

She said, "Are you worried about Miss Black? Maybe now is a good time to go see her. Hurry. Because I'm very eager for our date."

Williams choked on his soda when she said that. They couldn't help themselves and started laughing. I pulled her to the side and showed her the paper.

I said, "This is Samantha's info? You're telling me I should just go see her? Just like that?"

"Yes." She said it with such ease. She said, "Go talk to Miss Black. Show her you like her. Get rejected and come see me. Should I drive you?"

"Rejected? How do you know she'll reject me?"

She wrapped her arms around my neck and said, "Because you belong with me. Miss Black can't handle you and she knows that. I promise you. She'll push you away. Then we will go on a lovely date." She stepped away and motioned me to go.

She had another thing coming if she thought I'd ever go out with her. It was the push I needed to go see Samantha. I told my friends I would be back and left. I walked for about half an hour. Then I was in her neighborhood. Or so I thought. When I followed the addresses down, her house number didn't show up. It was skipped as if the house didn't exist. I couldn't understand it.

It took me a few blocks until I came to what

38

looked like a forest. It was at the end of the street and at first I thought it was just decoration or maybe a dead end. But when I went through it I found a long trail, filled with rocks. Beyond the trail was a grassy hill leading to a house. It had to be Samantha's home. The walk was quiet and peaceful. In a way, the whole scenery fit her.

It hit me that I was going to have to explain how and why I found her house. I couldn't lie and say I found it by accident because it was in a secluded area. It couldn't be the truth. She would have thought I was creepy if I told her I got her information from the office. I also didn't want to lie.

As I got close, I saw the home's design. It was an ordinary small two-story home with light blue paint. There was a small garage on the right side of the house but it was closed. The house was way up top and on the other side of a grassy hill. The trail I was on bordered the left side of the hill and went all the way up to Samantha's house.

I followed the trail up to the home's porch. Samantha came out as I got close and looked right at me. It was like she knew I was coming. I started looking around for video cameras. Her family must have been pretty wealthy.

She had that same look on her face. She didn't look happy, sad or anything. Her face was very plain. It was hard to tell what mood she was in. All I could really figure was that she was relaxed and sleepy. It looked like she had just woken up.I waved when I got close to her doorstep.

I said, "Samantha. Hey there. I know you're probably wondering what I'm doing here."

"No," she said. "I know why you're here."

"You do?"

She looked past me saying, "You got my address and came to see if I was ok." She still wasn't looking at me. "I'm fine. So you can leave." She went inside and started to close the door. I quickly ran to it and called her name.

I stopped the door saying, "Hey wait!"

She said, "What do you want?"

I had to think of something to say fast. She didn't seem to be in a chatty mood. Isabella was right. Samantha didn't want my company. But I wasn't going to give up easily.

"Well where've you been? You haven't been at school."

She said, "I have been. You just don't see me. Bye." She started to shut the door again.

"Samantha wait a minute! Don't close the door in my face like that."

She looked back and said, "Oh. Sorry. Do you mind stepping back?"

I said, "What do you mean you're at school? I never see you. So you haven't been expelled?"

She said, "Why would they expel me? You're being odd. Go home and get some sleep."

It started to feel like I was getting nowhere. Why was she so different than before? When I first met her she was polite and kind. Now she was the exact opposite. And she was slightly harsh.

I said, "Samantha look. I wanted to see if you were ok. Last week with Caroline and her friends. I'm sorry. It was because of me. Caroline is my ex and she's the jealous type. The very jealous type."

Samantha said, "She's the least of my worries. Trust me. I'm fine. Now goodnight."

"Wait!"

She opened it again. "Now what? What do you need?"

I couldn't think of anything better to say. I said, "Can I come inside?"

She smiled and politely said, "No. Goodnight."

"Samantha come on," I said. "I don't know what's changed since last week. But I liked sitting and talking with you. And to be honest I want to do that again. Right now. Can I come inside?"

To my surprise she stepped back and opened the door.

She said, "Fine. But no funny business, Thomas." I smiled when she turned away to walk inside. Samantha Black remembered my name. Had she thought about me since we last spoke? I walked inside and closed the door. It was completely dark. I couldn't see her, but I could hear her footsteps.

"Excuse the lack of light," she said. The lights came on. She said, "I just don't like a lot of it."

She was standing by a light switch. Her house was clean and spacious. It made me think of my grandparents' home. It was very old fashioned. There were old wooden shelves and glass cabinets with china inside of them. It looked like we were in some sort of dining room. There was a large table with a red cloth over it. A candlestick was in the middle of it.

"Wow," I said. "It's pretty antiqued here. I like it."

"What exactly did you want to do?" She asked.

I looked at her for a moment. Her tone was still stern. She was very proper and with her calm look, it was hard to tell how she was feeling. I thought she was upset.

She said "Would you like to watch television?"

She led me to the next room. It was even bigger and more old-fashioned. There was brown furniture surrounding an old tv set. It wasn't like the widescreen or plasmas I was used to. This one was on the floor but it was still big and it had an antenna. We sat in front of it on a couch as she turned it on with a remote.

I asked, "What do you like to watch?"

She said, "I'm not a huge enthusiast for the television. I don't even know how to turn the thing on," she fiddled with the remote, "I like reading and poetry. Walks along the trail you found outside are nice as well."

I smiled and said, "I saw the book you were reading. You even read during class. I love to write stories. You should read one of mine." As I smiled I saw her smile almost barely. It was like she was trying to hide it. It made me laugh a bit.

When she heard me laugh her smile was gone. She looked at me fast and said, "What's funny?"

"Sorry," I said. "It's just that's the second time I've ever seen you smile. You look so serious all of the time. Like right now. It's a nice smile, Samantha. Use it more." She raised her eyebrow. I asked, "What?"

She looked really confused. "You're very unusual," she said. She turned to the tv and finally managed to turn it on.

I said "Hey what do you mean by unusual? Are you calling me weird?"

She looked at me and simply said, "Yes."

"What? Yeah, well you're..." I caught myself, remembering how mean everyone was towards her. And what a lie it would have been to agree with them and say she *was* weird. The truth was Samantha was probably the most amazing person I had been around. Not even Caroline made me feel what she did. At that moment, I wanted to know what it was. She wasn't like anyone I had ever met. Even if she did insult me, I couldn't bring myself to attack her.

I got up and said, "I'll just leave then, Samantha. Listen don't let anything those kids say bother you. You're great and I like being around you. I just came to see if you were ok."

I made my way towards the dining room. She sat up and said, "Why are you so different from the rest of them? Why are you being so kind to me?" I turned to her. She continued, "You aren't like the others. They insult me and avoid me. But not you. You're polite and kind. Why?"

I shrugged, "I just don't see what's to insult or avoid. I hear what they say. But I just don't see it. So I can't bring myself to lie and conform with them. You're so different from everyone at school. I like it.

"Everyday is the same for me. I hadn't been to school in a while. I guess I was trying to get away from the breakup and the drama of school. I came back and I thought nothing had changed. But then I saw you and sat with you. Everything was so...different." I got closer to her. "Then we talked and shared that moment."

I sat down again and said, "I guess I came to see

what that was and if I could feel it again. Sometimes I just feel so trapped. It's like I don't belong. Like when I'm with my friends, hearing them laugh at people and make dumb jokes. It's not me. I feel out of place. With you though I felt so…simple you know? Free."

She smiled and looked away. She said, "You're sweet."

I said, "Last week you tried to kiss me. I'm sorry I overreacted. I was just surprised."

She said, "Kiss you?"

"Remember? You got really close to my face. Like this."

Just like it was in the café. The closer I got the hotter I became. The longer I was around Samantha the stronger that familiar yet unknown feeling got inside of me. I couldn't resist the urge. My lips were already pressing against her soft and moist mouth.

I brushed her long and red hair back behind her shoulders. It was so soft and flowing. My fingers couldn't have gotten caught if I wanted them to. She hid her brown eyes behind her eyelids as they closed. Her strong scent of sweet cherries rushed into my nose and I was captivated. She took in a deep breath and kissed me back. She put her hands on my back and got closer. Then out of the blue she quickly pulled away and pushed me.

"What do you think you're doing?" She said.

My senses were tense and I could barely think. I said, "I don't know. I just got taken away."

She wiped her mouth after catching her breath. She said, "I thought I told you no funny business. Did I not?"

"Samantha I'm sorry. I just. I don't know. I've thought about you all week and I can't understand why. I can't figure out why I like you so much."

I stopped talking. She took my face with both hands and kissed me. I wrapped my arms around her and kissed her back. It was unlike anything I had ever experienced. It was flurries of soft and firm kisses. The taste of sweet candy bit my tongue with each kiss. Constantly teasing me again and again. I couldn't get enough of her.

Just like she had done earlier, she stopped. This time she got off the couch after pushing me away. "It's time for you to leave," she said.

"What? What happened?" I got up and walked to her. She turned away from me as I tried to talk to her. We were at the door. "Samantha what's wrong," I said.

"Get out," she said coldly.

"Tell me what I did wrong! You kissed me back. You grabbed my face and pulled me in."

She said, "I know that! I like you too. I can't figure out why. You need to get out. Go home and don't *ever* come here again."

"You're making no sense, Samantha."

She stepped back as she crossed her arms. I walked to her as she looked away. Her hand was on the door, slowly opening it. "Get..."

I stopped her. I grabbed her hips and pulled her in. She met my lips and wrapped her arms around my neck. She didn't resist. Her kisses got stronger. She pushed me against the wall and leaned on me.

As I leaned in for another kiss, she pushed me against the wall. The pictures on the wall almost fell as she stepped back.

"Go home. Please go home, Thomas," she said. "Never come here again. Sorry."

I stared at her as she quickly ran away and up a staircase. I heard a door slam. I wasn't going to follow her without her saying it was ok. If I wanted to talk to her it would have to be at school. Yet again she left me puzzled.

What happened? She kissed me more than once and randomly pushed me away. She didn't come back downstairs for a while. I had no choice but to leave. Maybe I would see her at school.

3. Eyes

Monday came along and I hadn't talked to Samantha since Thursday night. I still didn't know what happened between us. Did or didn't she like me? Why did she pull me in then push me away like that?

She had returned to school but I never got the chance to speak to her. Whenever I saw her, she would quickly vanish. It was obvious that she was avoiding me. What did I do to upset her?

Isabella didn't let me forget our little *deal*. As soon as I got home that night she called me. I couldn't lie. I had to tell her the truth. Just like she predicted.

Samantha Black did reject me. I was forced to take Isabella Butler out. Surprisingly though, she wasn't bad company. She was actually pretty nice to be around. Now that I was dating her it seemed less annoying since she wasn't actually stalking me. We started spending a lot of time together.

"Wow. You sure can eat a lot," she laughed. "Would you like to try mine?"

I shook my head yes. We were having lunch at a

seafood buffet. I refused but she paid for everything again. It was hard for her not to grow on me. Isabella was really sweet and polite. She didn't let anyone mess with me either. I would have to be a real jerk not to appreciate her kindness. She fed me some of her lobster. It was my first time having it and it hit the spot.

"That tasted amazing!"

She laughed and clapped her hands. "Yes I know. I knew you would love it, my love. Here I'll let you have half."

She was sweet. It almost took my mind away from what happened the other night. But once we finished and started walking, my mind started to drift again. And Isabella was good at reading me. She had no problem with stating the obvious.

She said, "So how is Miss Green? Have you spoken to her."

I shook my head. "No. I just got over it. Talking to her about it doesn't seem smart. Besides she made her choice. She ended things."

She took my hand. She said, "Her lose, my love. Don't let it get to you. Besides. Is she really worth your thought if she made you hurt like that? I don't think so."

True. Caroline was partly to blame for my three months of depression. But it just didn't seem like her to just end things like that. She didn't explain it.

Since her family trip she had been acting different. She never used to distance herself the way she was.

Isabella said, "And Miss Black? How did things go? I still can't believe you kissed that creature." She laughed a bit. She said, "Sorry, love. I just can't see the attraction with that one."

I said, "I don't really want to talk about that either. I'm still confused about what happened. She pulled me in and pushed me away over and over. She's so confusing."

"Samantha Black has issues," she said. "Big ones. Just leave her alone and stay with me. Let me relax that handsome head of yours. You waste too much time on headaches."

Isabella was the only person who didn't really *hurt* me. In the past she had been annoying. But it was because I had no interest in dating her. Once I got to know her, she was pretty nice to be around. She didn't stress me out at all.

I held her close and kissed her. She giggled and hugged me tight.

I said, "You're right, Isabella. Thank you for being here for me."

"Don't worry about that, my love. I'm your guardian angel. I'll keep you far away from the monsters and close to the sunlight." She laughed again as I kissed her neck.

"Hey. Let's go to the pool party," I said. "I'm

supposed to meet up with my friends. I want to swim with you."

She kissed my cheek. "Anything for you. Let's go. But you do know Caroline will be there right? Are you ok with that?"

I shrugged. "It won't bother me. Come on." I kissed her again as we started walking.

We walked to Veronica's neighborhood. It was a quiet and overly expensive one. A lot of old and retired people lived there, so nothing bad ever happened. Once we were through the gate, we walked towards her house.

It was easy to tell which one was the party. Cars were crowded around her house and there were high school students everywhere. I'm sure the neighbors hated it.

Veronica's house was pretty big. In the back was the pool. I lead Isabella up the driveway and along the side of the house. I have no idea what was running through my mind when I suggested going. As soon as I saw Caroline with her friends I went from ten to zero fast.

Isabella squeezed my hand. "Don't let it bother you. Come. Let's sit."

She sat me down in a chair and sat on my lap. After wrapping her arms around me she got comfortable. It didn't bother me as much as it did on our first date. Isabella grew on me. She was good at getting me to laugh.

She said, "There's the handsome smile I adore so much."

"Thanks, Isabella," I laughed.

As we laughed my friends walked to us. They must have seen us walking in. They all looked crept out.

Martinez said, "You have got to be kidding me, man."

"You were serious when you said you two were dating?" Tylor asked.

Isabella smiled and said, "He can date whoever he wants. You four always try to give him girl advice. Where are *your* girlfriends? Idiots."

Martinez shot back. "Don't call me stupid you basket case!"

"Stop it guys," I said. "Not now. Yes I'm dating Isabella. Seriously don't you five start arguing. Let's just enjoy the party."

Isabella was the first to agree. "Ok, love. I'll take it easy. Hey wait here. I will go get you some punch." She got up and quickly walked towards the refreshments.

It was impossible not to feel the stares from my friends. Martinez said, "Dude. First the goth chick and now the stalker?"

"Neither one of them were invited." I looked back. It was Caroline talking. She looked incredible in her black swimsuit. I looked away to avoid getting drawn in by her looks. She told my friends to get lost so she could talk to me. They didn't question her at all. Once they left she sat on my lap.

"Caroline what are you doing?" I said.

She said, "Calm down. I hate standing and talking to someone who's sitting. Are you seriously here with Isabella Butler? You're off your game aren't you? Loners and stalkers? I didn't know they were your thing." She laughed lightly.

"Caroline get off of me and go away," I said.

She slapped my shoulder lightly. "Oh take a joke. You have to admit though. Isabella? I can see Samantha. But even you have told me how much Isabella creeps you out."

I looked back at Isabella. She was pouring drinks carefully. I looked back and sighed.

"It's complicated," I said. "And she's not bad company. She's pretty sweet."

"Well isn't that cute," she said. "Listen, Thomas. I really want to talk to you. I know I've been acting weird lately. I don't hate you and I never wanted to stop talking to you. I really care about you."

I said, "What? Where is this coming from? Couldn't you have said this last week when I came back? You really hurt me this summer. You went away for a while. When you came back the first thing you did was dump me."

She let out a heavy breath and tilted her head back. "Ugh. I know. You don't understand. I didn't really have a choice. It's complicated ok?"

"Let me hit you with something that's simple. Get off of him and get lost."

We looked to see Isabella in front of us. She was holding our drinks and glaring at Caroline.

She said, "You blew your chance with him. He's with me now. So get lost."

Caroline laughed. "He doesn't even like you. You're a rebound."

"Don't make me put these drinks down," Isabella said.

Before Caroline could say anything back I said, "Just go, Caroline. And don't talk to her like that. She didn't hurt me. You did. I don't want to talk about anything with you."

She said, "It's more complicated than you think. I didn't breakup with you to hurt you. Enjoy your date." She got up and turned to Isabella. She simply laughed and walked away. As Isabella sat with me Veronica stormed over.

"No way. No! Thomas take that weirdo out of here. She's not invited."

I said, "Veronica come on. She's not bothering anyone."

She said, "No! Get her out of here or I'll get both of you out of here."

Isabella said, "Touch him and you'll be sorry, Miss Bridges. Leave us alone. We're enjoying the moment."

Veronica shot Isabella a cold look then looked at me. Surprisingly she just turned away and stormed off. Isabella and I laughed about it until three guys came over. They were on the football team. It was Kendal, Greg and Patrick who came over.

They tormented me and my friends pretty much all of middle school and parts of high school. Caroline protected me from them during our relationship. But my friends weren't so lucky. Greg was the tallest but also the dumbest.

He said, "You have to leave, man. Isabella the weirdo is giving off too much creepy."

"It never ends," I sighed. "Can you guys just walk away like you don't see us?"

Patrick was the second in command. He was pretty built as well but not so intimidating.

He said, "Sorry, dude. Invite only. Besides you aren't even dressed to swim."

Isabella said, "Thomas can't swim and I'm petrified of large bodies of water. So…"

Greg interrupted her. He said, "No one's talking to you. Thomas, you two have to leave."

I said, "Let's just go Isabella." We got up and started walking away. But Isabella couldn't help herself. She just had to mouth off to them. It got to

55

Greg the most. And of course they weren't going to go after the small girl. They went after me.

Before I knew it all three of them had grabbed me. They picked me up and started walking me over towards the pool.

Greg said, "We tried to be nice. You should teach that weirdo not to run her mouth so much."

"Right I'm sorry!" I said. "I'll talk to her. Just don't throw me in there. Greg. I can't swim!"

They kept laughing as they carried me closer to the deep end. Isabella demanded they put me down over and over. But it was pointless. There were three of them and one of her. My friends tried to help as well. But they were too afraid of the jocks to actually do something.

My heart began to race. We were feet away from the pool. It was so deep. The sound of water splashing around began to frighten me. My friends were just standing there and shouting but not actually interfering. I realized that they weren't going to stop them. Before I could blink, I was in the air. I heard a splash and suddenly the water was to my neck as I struggled to stay afloat.

"Help!" I pleaded, "I can't swim! Help me!"

Greg only laughed and gave his friends high fives. The water was to my nose and I was deafened by the rush of water into my ears. I kicked and swatted. But I couldn't stop it. I had gone under and

I was sinking to the bottom. I screamed for help but cupped my mouth. I realized I lost all of my breath. My lungs started aching for air.

"Cough, cough."

I was drowning. It felt as if my head was going to explode as my chest ached. Then I was sleepy. I heard noises as I hit the bottom. Someone was standing at the surface looking at me. Caroline. I reached for her. Then everything went black.

It felt like I had been sleeping for years. I gasped for air as I felt the familiar touch of soft and moist lips. She was giving me air. It felt cold yet sweet. It had to be a dream. I coughed for a moment still thinking I was drowning. Then I felt her soft hands cupping mine.

"You're fine," she said. "Try to relax so your lungs can get more air."

I opened my eyes. For a moment I thought Caroline or Isabella had saved me. When my vision was clear, I saw that it was Samantha who was holding my hand. She was wearing black tight jeans and a white tank top with spaghetti straps. She was completely drenched but still looked breathtaking.

Suddenly I forgot I almost drowned.

I said, "Samantha?"

She said, "If I hadn't come, you would have drowned."

I said, "Wait. Have you been here this entire time? I didn't see you anywhere. When did you get here? Samantha?"

Her focus had left from me. Now it was on Caroline. I watched as Samantha's face filled with an obvious rage. She was pissed. Before I could say anything she was on her feet. She was walking towards Caroline.

Everyone stopped what they were doing. Samantha got face to face with her. Veronica stepped in front of her but was effortlessly pushed aside, into the pool. Samantha glared at Caroline.

Caroline said, "What do *you* want?"

Samantha shouted, "Are you out of your mind? Those three almost killed him! If I hadn't come he would be dead. Don't you have any sense at all?"

Samantha's hands had balled into fists. If it had ever been hard to tell her mood it wasn't then. She looked as if she was ready to thrash Caroline. Even Caroline looked nervous. She took a single step back, but Samantha followed with a step of her own. Suddenly Caroline was as stiff as a statue.

"Keep your friends away from him. And I don't want *you* near him. Do you understand?"

Caroline didn't even answer her. I had never seen her that shaken up. Quickly I rushed to them and grabbed Samantha's hand.

"Hey. Samantha I'm fine. Samantha!"

She looked at me. Caroline suddenly stumbled back as she started breathing again. She caught herself from falling. Before Samantha could think about confronting her again, I lead her out of the pool party. She seemed to know exactly where to go. She walked with me all the way to the driveway. She had to have been there before I was.

"Samantha are you alright?" I turned her to me. She was drenched. I took my shirt off and began wiping her down gently. "I can't believe you jumped in fully clothed like that. Did you ruin your cell phone?"

"I don't own one and I'm fine," she said.

"Have you been here this whole time? Why are you avoiding me?"

She said, "I have to go. You should get into some heat. You'll catch a cold."

As she walked past me I grabbed her hand. I said, "So will you. Stop and talk to me." I got in front of her and looked at her. It was impossible not to be taken by her beauty. Her energy was shrouding me and in an instant I got that rush again. But I tried to stay focused.

I said, "Why are you avoiding me? Did I hurt you or anything the other night?"

She shook her head. "Of course not. I can barely control myself around you. You're so different."

I took her other hand and got close. " Then why are you avoiding me, Samantha?"

I couldn't help it. I pressed my lips against hers softly. She took my hands and closed her lips on mine. Our tongues said hello for the first time. Her kisses reminded me of the winter. So refreshing, calm and delicate. The taste of cherries danced on my tongue again, refusing to let me stop kissing her. I held her hips and pressed her soft body against mine.

I thought things were going way better than Tuesday. Then she did the same thing again. She suddenly stopped and pushed me away. She wiped her mouth and caught her breath. I didn't know what to say. I just watched her for a moment.

She scoffed. "Learn how to swim." Then she just walked off. I reached for her hand but she snatched it away. She turned to me and said, "No. Get it through your skull. We can't be together. So leave me alone. Don't follow me. I don't want to be anywhere near you. So stop obsessing over me."

Obsessing? Damn. Now that hit a soft spot. I couldn't say a word. She was more than harsh this time. She was being cruel. But it felt so plastic. As if she was going against her feelings.

"Hate to say I told you so."

Isabella got beside me and took my hand. She said, "Miss Black wants nothing to do with you.

Sorry, love. Trust me. It's her not you."

Samantha had stopped walking as soon as she heard Isabella's voice. Her back was still to me. But it was painfully obvious she was listening. So I got an idea. If Samantha liked me, that meant I could make her jealous.

I turned to Isabella and said, "Hey. Do you want to go out? Right now. Just us."

Samantha turned her ear towards as. Her back was still toward me but I knew it was working.

Isabella got excited and giggled. "Another date. Right now? Of course, love! Anything you want. What do you want to do?"

I put my arm around her shoulder and began walking. We were walking towards Samantha.

I said, "Oh I don't know. Hey. Why don't you pick *babe*." That's when Samantha turned to me. She looked annoyed not pissed. I rose my eyebrow at her as if saying, "What?"

"Don't give me that look. What do you think you're doing?" She said. She walked to me and removed my arm from Isabella.

I shouted, "Samantha what's your problem?"

Isabella said, "Yes, Miss Black." She wrapped her arms around me and lifted one leg. "What is the problem? You can't be with him."

Samantha said, "You're getting with her? You can't take her to the movies like that."

61

I said, "You can't tell me what to do. Besides why do you care?"

She said, "You clearly like me. Why are you using her to get to me?"

Isabella said, "For your information I already know he likes you. I'm the one who told him to come see you and gave him your address. I want him to see how you won't let him hold your hand. So he will never let go of mine. Go on. Tell him you can't be with him."

Samantha grabbed my hand and pulled me to the side. She said, "Can you not see how *crazy* that girl is? Why are you hanging out with her? You shouldn't be with someone like Isabella."

I said, "Samantha why do you care so much? You keep pulling me in and pushing me away. You don't get to say who I can be with besides you. Is that possible or is Isabella right?"

She hesitated to speak. She looked away and said, "We can't be together. She's right. But Thomas you can't be with her either. You don't even like her."

I pushed her away gently saying, "This time I'm pushing *you* away Samantha. Goodbye."

I walked away from her, grabbed Isabella's hand and lead her away. I ignored Samantha's protest until we were too far away to hear her. It worked. I made her jealous meaning she liked me. But why did she let me walk away? I couldn't understand. I brushed it out of my mind and took Isabella to a movie theater.

She drove us to the Demerra Theater. It was one of the more popular movie theaters in our city. The inside was huge and besides movie rooms, it had a large arcade. After we got our tickets we went to a dance machine. Everything was fine up until I thought I was seeing Samantha over and over.

One moment I thought she was at the popcorn counter or by a water fountain. When I looked to see, there would be someone else there. I felt like I was losing my mind. Even when I turned away it felt like I was being watched. It felt like she was right there looking me in the eyes. But every time I looked around me she was nowhere to be seen.

The movie finally began after half an hour. Isabella got popcorn and bought me a hotdog. With food, her and the hilarious movie, my mind got occupied enough to forget about Samantha.

But the feeling didn't leave. It was like some sixth sense. It felt like someone was watching me. My insides would ring like some alarm. I turned to the exits repeatedly. But she was never there.

Isabella laughed hysterically at the film. It was a movie about two men who were pretending to be cops. It made me laugh a few times. But not enough to help me ignore the bells. I looked back once more. Finally I caught her. Not completely but I saw a shadow quickly move away from the light. Samantha was there and it pissed me off. Now *she* was stalking me?

I smiled and leaned to Isabella. I whispered, "Hey. I need to use the restroom. I'll be back."

She smiled and said, "Ok. But hurry. You're going to miss it!"

I quickly made my way out of the theater. Samantha wasn't at the exit. I stormed out of the room and looked around. I was starting to think my mind was playing tricks on me. Then someone grabbed my arm. It made me flinch a bit as I looked back. It was her.

I said, "Samantha! Have you been watching and following me?"

She said, "Why are you here with that witch? I told you not to go out with her! How can you kiss one girl and take out another?"

"You aren't my parent! And you can't tab me like I'm some book. So stop following and watching me like I'm yours."

She said, "So I guess you would have preferred me letting you drown? No one was going to jump in! I saved your life!"

I grabbed her face and kissed her. She grabbed my wrists but slowly gave in. I held her in my arms as we got against a wall. I started running my hands through her ruby red locks. The smell of sweet cherries never got old. The longer I was around her the more hypnotic she got. She pulled her lips away but I held onto her.

"Why," I said. "Why do you do this?"

She looked sad. She said, "Because I like you. I really, really like you. I can't help myself when you're so close. That's why I have to put so much space between us."

I said, "So then you save my life, stalk me, tell me who I can and can't be with? Samantha just let me be around you. You could be the one in that theater."

She looked away saying, "I wish I could be. But I can't. My family and I moved here for a reason. We don't need more trouble."

"Trouble? I won't cause you any trouble at all."

She shook her head and pulled away. "Yes. Yes you would. I need to go and you need to go home. Leave that girl alone."

"Samantha you have no right to do this to me," I said firmly. "I'll be with who I want. Now go home." I turned away. When I walked I bumped right into her.

She said, "Listen to me. Stay. Away. From her. I'm warning you to go home and leave her alone."

I said, "Yeah? And what if I don't, Samantha? What will you do?"

She looked away and scoffed. "You are being

really stupid right now. Just listen to what I'm saying. Even if it sounds weird. Leave her alone. It's time to go."

She took my hand and started dragging me to the exits. For a girl she was pretty strong. I could see why Caroline had trouble breaking her grip. Even I couldn't pull away. She led me outside and finally let me go. She pointed south.

"Home. Go right now. I'm not leaving you with her."

I said, "Are you this controlling with every guy you date? No wonder you're single."

She said, "One, we're not dating. Two, I'm single by choice."

I laughed saying, "Yeah my friend Ace says that all of the time. It's called denial. You're controlling, withdrawn and pretty cold to be honest. You won't get any friends being that way."

She walked to me and got in my face. "You need to watch the way you speak to me. You have no idea what my life is about. I'm aware that I have no friends." She looked away. Her voice got soft as she spoke, "They all hate me. It doesn't take a genius to see that."

I felt incredibly awful. For the first time she looked as if she could cry. She always acted so calm and impassable. It felt like she couldn't be hurt.

I held her arms. I said, "Hey. Samantha I'm

sorry. I shouldn't have said that."

"Get off of me," she said.

"Samantha. All I ever wanted to be was someone who didn't make your life Hell at school. That's why I sat by you. But I never imagined that I'd fall so hard for you."

She said softly, "Let got. Please. You have to get back. Get off and step back." She sounded tired.

"Samantha I can't be another person who leaves you by yourself. I can't. I care about you."

She looked at me smiling with her eyes half shut. When I saw her eyes I gasped and stepped back. Before I could focus she took my hands and pulled me close. Her grip was stronger than before and her kiss was hard.

Hard yet so electric. The rush of cold ecstasy rushed from my mouth to my toes over and over. I could barely keep up with her pace.

She kept kissing and backing me up until I was against a wall. There was no one around us under the night sky. Samantha kept squeezing my hands until they started to ache. I tried pulling away but she had me against the wall and she was strong.

I finally caught my breath as she started kissing my face. "Samantha," I said. "Whoa."

"I tried to warn you," she whispered. "Forgive me. I can't stop." She kept kissing my cheek. Then bit me.

I quickly flinched back. "Hey. Samantha take it easy you…"

I was frozen stiff. I was holding both of her wrists but I couldn't stop staring at the redness of her eyes. They weren't brown anymore. As the moonlight beamed I saw her eyes glow like rare rubies. She was smiling wide, her eyes were slightly shut and she had fangs. I couldn't believe what I was seeing.

I stuttered, "Samantha. Your eyes."

She got close and whispered into my ear, "I want to tell you a secret. Promise not to tell a soul. Or I might have to kill you."

"Kill…me?"

She broke my grip with no effort at all. Black smoke suddenly appeared as she vanished from my eyesight. She quickly appeared right beside me with her back against the wall.

She kissed my cheek and said, "Do you want to know? Do you want to hear my secret?"

What was she? I wasn't afraid but, I couldn't tell if she was dangerous or not. Suddenly she wasn't the quiet and soft Samantha. Besides the fangs and red eyes, her personality had shifted. It seemed so…dark. She laughed a little and got face to face with me.

She said, "What's wrong? Do you think I'm going to hurt you?"

Without any warning she vanished and black smoke appeared where she stood.

"Oh, looooove." It was Isabella singing. I looked to see her walking out of the theater. She saw me but tiptoed to me. Then she pounced on me saying, "What are you up to? Are you bored with the movie?"

I looked in every direction. But Samantha was nowhere to be found...or seen. I didn't know if she was still there or not. Isabella clearly hadn't seen what I did. She came out right after Samantha turned into smoke. I decided not to say a word to Isabella, remembering Samantha's words.

"I want to tell you a secret. Promise not to tell a soul. Or I might have to kill you."

4. Prey

Two weeks had passed since my night with Samantha. She seemingly went missing again. Since that night I didn't know if she was gone or just staying out of sight. I would look for her everywhere. My eyes constantly searched the back of the classrooms and my ears would desperately listen for laughter.

Whenever I heard it, I looked hoping it was laughter towards Samantha Black. If she was at school I wasn't catching any sights of her. My mind couldn't grasp what happened that night. I still couldn't believe it. She turned to smoke. One minute she was there then the next, black smoke appeared out of nowhere and she vanished. Then those eyes.

They were red. I was sure of it, but I couldn't believe it. Samantha told me she wasn't normal, but now I knew she wasn't talking about the kids thinking she was weird. It was deeper than that. I tried my best to stop thinking about that night.

But I felt her presence everywhere I went. I could feel her eyes watching my every move. My mind would trick me into believing she was sitting in the café at lunch or standing in the crowds during passing periods. But then she would vanish when I focused in her direction.

On a Thursday morning, I was in the school library. It was a large and nice place to focus. Not too many students ever went there. So it was like a ghost town filled with bookshelves. That's where I went to clear my mind. Mostly I buried myself with work to avoid the thoughts. But they haunted me.

Samantha lingered in my mind. The more I tried to figure her out, the more I worried. I couldn't forget what she said. She had said, *"I want to tell you a secret. Promise not to tell a soul. Or I might have to kill you."*

Those words played over and over again in my head. Constantly I would look over my shoulder for her. Would she actually kill me? I obviously wasn't supposed to see what I did.

That morning I was working on notes for my exams. It was open book. I would have had to be an idiot to not pass. As I wrote my notes I felt someone coming from the hall. I could see Samantha in my mind. Her smile was wide and her eyes were glowing red.

I sat up straight in my chair, as the footsteps got

louder. I finally took a breath when I saw it was only Tylor and Williams. I had never been so glad to see them. It made me feel somewhat safer with other people around. Although I doubt the teachers or my friends could do anything to whatever Samantha was. It hit me that she may have been more than human. She had to be.

My friends were watching me strangely. They looked oddly suspicious. When they sat down they waited for a few seconds. Then Tylor spoke.

He said, "Fine I'll break the ice. Thomas, what's going on between you and the new girl?"

"Yeah," Williams said. "You haven't talked to us since you started hanging out with her. Where is she?"

I didn't look at them. I said, "I'm not Samantha's keeper. I haven't seen her either. Most likely she transferred for obvious reasons."

I didn't believe that at all. I knew Samantha was somewhere. I had the same feeling I had at the theater. She was far away or close. But still watching me. Listening to every word I spoke. It made my spine stiffen as I felt my sweat run down my face. As I wrote my notes, my pencil tip broke.

Tylor persisted, "You're lying. We never see you anymore and you hardly ever hangout now. You're always with Samantha."

"I don't know!" I said. The librarian shushed me.

I was losing my grip and it wasn't even because of my friends. The suspence of Samantha's whereabouts and scope on me was driving me insane.

Was or wasn't she there? Every time I tried to ignore it she would pop up in my mind again. I would see her eyes and hear her voice. Kill me? Was she going to kill me?

The sick and twisted part was that I missed her. I still liked her. I could still feel her soft body against me. She was so beautiful and quiet. Her beauty didn't demand attention and she wasn't overly confident. The way her touch felt so different from everyone else's. It took me away to some sort of wonderland. With her gone I was missing that feeling.

I fought my feelings. I could still hear her words.

"I want to tell you a secret. Promise not to tell a soul. Or I might have to kill you."

On top of these mixed feelings of fear, nervousness and desire, my friends were still pestering me. Samantha was the last person I wanted to talk about.

Tylor started begging. He said, "Thomas come on. No one has seen you lately. We miss you. Just tell us the truth. Are you with her?"

Williams added, "What about Caroline? Last month you were missing school and depressed because of her. Now we barely…"

I lost it. I stood up and slammed my hands down. "I DON'T KNOW!"

It got really quiet. I looked around to see everyone staring at me. I stood there trying my best not to lose my mind. A redheaded girl shushed me and I thought it was Samantha. I gasped and nearly screamed, but it was someone else. Everyone in the library had still been watching me and there was more shushes. I took a deep breath to try and relax. I took my seat.

I explained, "I haven't seen or heard from Samantha in two weeks. She sort of followed me to the theater. I was there with Isabella."

Tylor and Williams both gasped at once. Tylor said, "Whoa. Now you have *two* stalkers."

"She followed you?" Williams asked.

"Kind of. But it's not like I really cared that she was there," I said. "I like Samantha a lot. She's just so…different."

Williams asked, "How?"

I ignored him and started scribbling on my notes. I was pretending to be busy, hoping they would leave. They wouldn't believe me if I told them what happened. I still didn't believe it. Samantha also told me not to tell anyone anything. Or she would kill me. My chest suddenly started to ache and I choked.

Williams started patting my back. He said,

"Whoa. You stopped breathing and spaced out. Are you alright?"

I shook my head. "I'm fine. I just swallowed my spit wrong."

"But you're shaking. Are you…"

I interrupted him. "I said I'm fine! Seriously. Please. I just want to study."

They shook their heads and got up. Tylor said, "Well we'll just go grab lunch. Are going to join us?" I shook my head no.

He said, "Oh. Well, hey we're having movie night tonight so don't bail on us again." I shook my head as they walked away. With Samantha in my mind I couldn't even get an appetite.

After I studied for an hour I left to take my exam in math. It was an easy test even without notes. The class was quiet and somewhat full. My eyes peered around to see the occasional passing of answers.

As I turned back, Samantha seemingly appeared in the back where she normally sat. It looked like she was gazing me. I turned back as fast as I could to catch her again. But it was someone else.

The teacher said, "Eyes on your own paper or you will receive a zero." I turned back around and continued my test. Samantha kept floating in my mind, but now she had shiny red hair and glowing eyes. How could anyone have red eyes? And how could a person just burst into smoke and disappear?

Wasn't she just a normal, human girl?

"I want to tell you a secret. Promise not to tell a soul. Or I might have to kill you."

Was that her secret? Not being human? And would she really kill me for seeing what she really was? Part of me thought so. But if that were true she would have killed me when she had the chance.

But a week had gone by and she had yet to do anything. And from what I could tell, Samantha liked me. But her eyes, teeth and grin kept flashing through my mind. It felt like she was right there in front of me.

But I knew better. She wasn't there. Somehow she was watching me without me being able to see her. Or I was going insane. I focused as hard as I could on my exam.

I finished first with ease and once class ended I was more than ready to go home. I handed my test to the teacher and left. I didn't even bother going to my locker.

I walked through the crowds of students, constantly looking over my shoulder. My mind wasn't playing tricks on me. I knew she was there. But when I looked she was vanishing. Samantha Black was stalking me in the shadows. Why? My heart started to race as I sped up. Every time I looked forward it felt like she was getting closer and closer. Her heavy presence was shrouding me.

"Promise not to tell a soul. Or I might have to kill you."

I hadn't said anything to anyone. There was no reason for her to kill me. But then why was she hunting me? Why was she stalking me and refusing to be caught? I imagined her turning into smoke, seeing her red eyes and sharp teeth.

Did she like me or did she want to kill me? The more I thought about it the more I started to get scared shitless. Before I knew it, I was running down the halls. I pushed through everyone, trying to get far away fast.

It felt like I was being chased. Even with the hundreds of kids around me, I felt like some prey in a forest. I was all alone, defenseless and weak, hoping and praying that the predator didn't catch me in its teeth. I looked back to see if she was there. Suddenly my foot slipped and I was on my face. Quickly I shuffled and crawled against a locker. I looked left then right. I felt trapped with nowhere to run. I could hear her laugh ringing in my head.

"Promise not to tell a soul. Or I might have to kill you."

I held my head, trying to fight off the visions and her voice. I quickly jerked back when someone touched my shoulder. But it was only Caroline.

She said, "Um. This is probably a dumb question. But are you alright? I saw you running. Then you fell." She sat beside me. "What's up?"

I said, "Nothing. I'm just in a hurry to get home."

She said, "Right. So why do you look like you've seen a ghost? And you're shaking."

I looked at my hands. They were covered in sweat and shaking as if I had some fever. Caroline took them and said, "What's going on? You've been acting really weird lately."

"Nothing, Caroline. I just need to get home. Exams are stressing me out. I'm pretty sure I failed my exam and it's going to ruin my gpa." I stood up.

She stood up with me. "You're freaking out over grades? You have straight A's. I know when you're lying, Thomas. Tell me what's bothering you."

"I'm tired and I want to go home," I said. "Excuse me." I walked around her and headed towards the exits.

She caught up and said, "Fine. Go into your little shell. But can I talk to you for a few minutes? It's important."

"I really don't want to talk," I said.

She grabbed my shoulder and turned me to her. She said, "Stop and let me talk. I realize your weird girlfriend has made you forget about me. But I still care about you."

"Caroline you're the one who broke up with me. Remember? You were cold about it and never explained it."

She said, "I know. I just don't know how to open up to you. The breakup was hard for me too ok? I think about you all of the time. I miss everything we used to do."

I shook my head. "No. It's too late for that. You can't do this. Not now."

She followed me saying, "Listen to what I have to say Thomas! We've known eachother for eighteen years. We can't just throw that away. Stop walking and listen to me!"

I stopped. We were outside near the parking lot curb. I held my head and let out a deep breath. She was right. Eighteen years was a lot of time. Even though she really hurt me.

She said, "Are you going to see your girlfriend now? Has she made you forget all about me then? Has that redheaded freak made you forget about our friendship?"

Samantha? She was talking about Samantha? Isabella was the closest I had to a girlfriend. But Caroline was talking about Samantha Black. She got frustrated with my silence.

She said, "Why her? Out of all of the pretty girls at our school, you go and pick the odd apple. She's so...strange. Those eyes. I can't wrap my mind around the way she stared at me. It really got to me. She has these eyes that strike this strange fear into you. It felt like snakes were just coiling around me as I stared into this bottomless pit. There's nothing there. She's…"

I held her arms and said, "Caroline. I'm dating Isabella. Not Samantha. I haven't seen her since our little pool incident."

She crossed her arms and turned away. At least she looked remorseful.

She said, "Blame Veronica for that one. I had nothing to do with it. I thought Isabella was going to jump in, but she was too afraid of the water. Before I knew it, Samantha had you in her arms on the ground. I never even saw her jump in."

That was my proof. I wasn't the only one who noticed her eyes or how fast she appeared than disappeared. She said, "And what's with you and these weird girls? Date someone normal for once."

I interrupted, "You think there's something wrong with every girl I like. You've been like that since we were little. You don't like any girls who like me."

She laughed, "Because you always pick weirdoes! But hey I liked Kimberly Cloverfield. Remember her? I was the one who set you up with her."

I said, "Caroline that was in middle school. Didn't you scare her half to death or something?"

She laughed, "She made fun of your hair one day and it made me mad. So I took her to the cave and gave her a little scare. Lots of bats in there."

I laughed and nudged her. "You scare off every girl who comes near me. Even before you came here, you'd chase off my crushes. It didn't stop until we got together freshman year."

She leaned on me. She said, "We've known eachother for a pretty long time. Haven't we, Thomas?"

I stepped away and said, "Since we were small kids. That's why the breakup hurt so badly. I don't even want to talk about it. So if that's what this talk is about, just don't."

She said, "I'm sorry, Thomas. Listen, maybe I should tell you why I did it. I'm not even supposed to tell you this but. Ha. You aren't even going to believe this but here it goes. You see I…"

I stopped her. She looked guilty. It was hard not to feel sorry for her. But I wasn't going to reopen the wound I had just shut.

She pleaded, "But it's very important. I was afraid to tell you, but right now you're hardly in my life. I would rather tell you and…"

I said, "I can't, Caroline. I'm sorry."

I started walking away as she said, "Have you noticed anything strange about her?"

That made me stop. Strange? Did she mean the redness of her eyes or the teeth? Or maybe the smoke? No. There wasn't anyway Caroline would have known.

I looked back as she said, "There's something strange about her. Maybe I'm just paranoid but when I'm close to her my senses just rattle. I would be careful around her if I were you."

I felt someone grab my hand. It was Isabella's. She smiled politely and said, "Don't worry about him, Miss Green. That's not your job anymore. It's mine. I don't appreciate your efforts to get back with him."

Caroline said, "I'm his friend and I've known him way longer than you have!"

Isabella said, "You've also hurt him way more than I have. If you were such a good friend you wouldn't have hurt him would you?"

"Isabella shut-up! It's way more complicated than that. Thomas can we please talk? Let me tell you why I broke up with you. It's really private though. I won't tell you while she's here."

I said, "Caroline I'm sorry. Maybe some other time. I forgot that I promised her a date tonight."

She said, "Fine. But I'm talking to you later whether you like it or not. I do still care about you."

I nodded as Isabella pulled me away. I couldn't stop thinking about Samantha Black and what she planned to do with me. Then there was Caroline. Isabella was the only person who didn't add to the stress.

She said, "Wow. These pretty monsters can't

keep their claws off you huh, love?"

I laughed as we got into the car. She drove while I sat back and relaxed. Isabella rubbed my head. She said, "Are you ok? Here. Have some water." She handed me a bottle of water. I was really glad she was so supportive.

Without her I wasn't sure how I would have stayed sane. She seemed like the perfect angel. She had her moments but overall she meant well. The quiet and peaceful drive helped me fall asleep.

5. Isabella's Diary

A gust of wind ran a cold chill over my body. When I opened my eyes I saw the moon in the night sky as leaves blew all around me. It felt like some strange dream.

When the wind hit me again I quickly sat up. I was lying on the ground in some strange pentagram. Candles were arranged on each star point of the pentagram. I was still drowsy.

"What the heck?" I said. "Isabella? Isabella!"

"Calm down, my love. You're safe. I promise."

I looked ahead. It was so blurry. I thought there was five of her. My eyes finally focused and I saw her sitting on the ground. She had her black diary beside her. She was sewing something in her hands as she read from the book.

"I'm glad you're finally awake, my love. Forgive my attitude from earlier. Those girls just make me jealous is all. They're so damned persistent. It sickens me."

I tried getting up but I felt incredibly weak and

dizzy. I dropped as quickly as I stood. I looked around to see all sorts of trees and bushes. Behind me was a cliff leading to a large lake. Somehow we had ended up on a cliff side surrounded by a large forest. For some reason I felt trapped.

"Some girls just don't get boundaries. Why can't they just let us be in peace? Why do these filthy monsters keep chasing you, my love?"

She sounded strange. Her tone was still polite but something was off. Somehow she seemed different. And dark.

She said, "You made me do this, Thomas. I didn't want to, but you made me. You've been a very naughty boy. Now I must put a leash on you. I'm so sorry." She giggled.

She kept sewing the thing in her hand. I could see it now. It was a doll. The more I watched the more crept out I got. The doll looked like me. I looked at the pentagram around me. Suddenly my heart dropped as this cold and dark fear swallowed me whole. Witchcraft. Isabella was performing some strange ritual on me. But that stuff wasn't real. It couldn't be.

I said, "Isabella...what are you doing?"

She finally looked at me. She had this deranged smile. Her eyes were wide and scary.

She giggled saying, "I'm making you behave of course. I can't have you going around kissing girls can I? I can't have you go holding other girls can I? No. You belong to me. You're mine. Only mine!"

She shouted then suddenly stopped. Her voice kept going from loud and angry to soft and polite. Then she was giggling hauntingly like some deranged schoolgirl. Her pace with her sewing sped up. She looked at me smiling and saying, "Oh. You thought I didn't see? You thought I hadn't seen you share tongues with Miss Black? No. Isabella sees everything. All things. Yes you've been a bad, bad boy."

I slowly started crawling away. I said, "Isabella. Please. Don't do anything you'll regret. Let's just talk."

She stood up. She shouted, "Talk? You want to talk? No talking. No, not now. Now you obey. Obey me, my love. I will make you behave. Miss Black will not have you. She will NOT HAVE YOU!"

I covered my ears as her scream echoed throughout the forest. As soon as the winds stopped blowing I could hear her laughing. Slowly I started backing out of the circle as she laughed uncontrollably. When I turned to run my body jerked backwards into the circle again.

"Don't run from me! Sit, boy!"

My body moved on its on. No matter how hard I resisted, my legs walked me to the center of the circle. Isabella giggled and said, "Sit boy." An incredibly strong force brought me to my knees. Isabella laughed with excitement.

She clapped and giggled, "Good, boy. Good!"

I couldn't move. She was holding the doll to her chest. She was hugging it close as she pet its head. I could feel the hairs on top of my head move as if someone was running their fingers through my hair. I brushed it off frantically and looked around but no one was in the circle with me.

She said, "Now you will never misbehave. You're mine. Only mine. And if you disobey me I will punish you."

I felt a sharp pain on my cheek. I grabbed my face and flinched away. Blood was on my hand. It felt like someone slashed me across the face with a knife. Isabella kept laughing. I looked to see her holding the needle to the doll's face.

She said, "Naughty boys get punishments. That was for kissing Miss Black. This is for letting Miss Green sit on your lap!" She slashed the doll. Instantly another cut split open on my face.

She said, "This is for holding Miss Black close to your body!" Another slash. More cuts began ripping open on my face.

"Isabella stop! Stop it!" I pleaded.

She cocked her head to the left. "Stop? You want me to stop? I'm only doing this because I love you. How else will you learn your lesson? I can't reward bad behavior!"

She started cutting the doll over and over. More and more cuts started to split open all over my body. I had no choice but to try and run away. As soon as I did my body rose from the ground and slammed back into the pentagram. I ached all over but still tried to escape.

Isabella said, "I loved you. I never wanted to resort to this. But I had no choice! You made me do this. This is the only way to keep you away from Miss Black! And Miss Green! And all of those other whores you love so much!"

She started twisting the doll's arm. I felt my arm slowly rise. I could hear the bone slowly crack. Then my arm twisted and my shoulder snapped. I couldn't hold in the pain. I dropped to my knees and screamed as I held my broken arm. It was completely useless. All I could move were its fingers.

Isabella cried, "It's for your own good! This will teach you not to sleep around. I will kill you before I let you cheat on me. You hear me? I will KILL YOU."

I quickly looked and saw her raise the needle into the sky. She was going to stab me. I quickly got on my feet and raced at her.

"No. NO DON'T," I pleaded.

She screamed, "No one will have your heart but

ME!"

She slammed the needle down. But her body flung backwards before the needle could pierce the doll. I hit the ground as she dropped the doll. I heard Isabella screaming as her body rolled along the ground. Quickly she got on her feet and glared my way.

She giggled and said, "So the fiend came to play?"

"Fiend?" I said.

I felt her eyes watching me and looked back. Samantha was standing close. Her long and red hair gleamed crimson as the wind blew against it. Her fists were balled and she was glaring at Isabella. I couldn't believe it. But at the same time I wasn't surprised. "Samantha?" I said.

She had her calm look. She said, "Thomas. That secret I wanted to tell you. Can I tell it to you now?" She looked at me and grinned. Her eyes were shining red underneath the moonlight. I swallowed a large lump in my throat as I shook my head.

Quickly she turned to Isabella as she crouched down. She held her hands out as sharp claws came from her fingertips. She said, "I'm a bloodsucking monster!"

In an instant she vanished as black smoke appeared again. I quickly looked to see her appearing close to Isabella. I could barely catch her movement. With one swipe to the face, she sent Isabella flying backwards. Isabella toppled over again and again until her body slammed into a tree. Before she could recover Samantha ran to her, grabbed her face and threw her. Her speed was nearly impossible to follow and her strength was monstrous.

Isabella landed on her feet but the force must have been too much. She tripped and kept rolling backwards. She managed to stop her toppling and caught her balance. She watched Samantha carefully while moving slowly.

Isabella said, "This is perfect. Now I can have the pleasure of getting rid of you myself. I've wanted you dead since the moment you moved here, daywalker."

Quickly she sprinted towards Samantha. Samantha swiped at her but missed as Isabella rolled out of the way. She grabbed her black diary from the ground and quickly jumped away. She flipped through the pages fast as Samantha turned to her.

She laughed and said, "It's over, daywalker!" She chanted words I couldn't understand. Suddenly she opened her mouth and breathed a giant ball of fire. I was yards away but I could still feel the intense heat from the flames. The stream of fire blitzed through a quarter of the forest and incinerated everything in its path.

I screamed for Samantha. Isabella was laughing hysterically. She stopped when she saw the silhouette standing in the flames. Samantha was completely unharmed.

She said, "Was that meant for me? You were way off. Run away, witch. You can't honestly believe you stand a chance against one of the tainted."

Isabella laughed. "A pure demon? No. But a half-blood shouldn't be hard for me to kill. Impure bloods can't hold against my magic. NOW DIE!"

She raised her hand and fired green lightning at Samantha. It shot her body and began electrocuting her. Samantha quickly flinched back and started screaming like a wild animal. I covered my ears as the winds started blowing fiercely. The ground was trembling. It was as if the forest was afraid of Samantha.

Isabella kept firing magic at Samantha as she laughed. She said, "Yes! Die, daywalker! Nothing will come between him and I. Nothing!"

I screamed for her to stop as Samantha screamed in agony. She was screaming to the sky then suddenly stopped. She looked at Isabella and grinned. Isabella shuddered and backed away as if she had seen a ghost.

"What?" Isabella said. "No. Impossible!" She fired more magic at Samantha. A gigantic bolt of lighting formed around Samantha as Isabella used both hands. Samantha grunted and started fighting the pain. She took a single step towards Isabella. Then another. Isabella slowly stepped back.

She said, "She's resisting my magic? No! It's not possible."

She fired more magic. Samantha let out a monstrous cry and suddenly the lightning stopped as this red static shot from Samantha's body like fireworks. The aftershock blew Isabella backwards. Steam was coming from Samantha's body but she kept grinning as she walked towards Isabella. She grabbed the black book and ripped it in two.

Isabella let out a painful scream. It was as if she had been stabbed through the heart. She got on her knees as Samantha threw away both halves.

She said, "They must not have taught you much about curses huh, witch? Your level of magic is useless against me. Get out of here. Next time I won't be so nice."

Samantha vanished and appeared near me. I was still on my knees as she looked down at me. She shook her head and said, "I told you to stay away from that witch."

I said, "I had no idea you actually meant she *was* a witch."

She bent down to me. She said, "Of course you didn't. You're not supposed to know. Give me your shoulder. Is it broken?"

"Yeah. She did something with a doll."

She looked at me and spat up blood. A gash slowly tore open on her throat. Slowly she stood up and we could hear Isabella giggling. Samantha turned to her. She had a doll that looked just like Samantha.

Isabella said, "Look, daywalker. It's my most powerful magic trick. Voodoo. Check this out."

Samantha's arms rose. Her left shoulder twisted back fast. There was a hideous snapping noise. Samantha let out a painful cry as Isabella snapped her right arm. There was nothing she could do. She was completely defenseless against the magic.

I shouted, "Isabella stop!" I ran to Samantha and held her in my arms. I said, "Can you talk?"

She said softly, "Run away. It's not safe."

I said, "Samantha I won't leave you."

"But you…" She stopped talking. Blood from the gash Isabella gave my face fell on Samantha's lip. I saw eyes nearly pop from her head as she took in a large sniff. She licked it with her tongue. Her back arched and she gasped as if coming from beneath water.

Isabella said, "It get's much worse for, Miss Black." She held the doll by the hair in her left hand. Samantha slowly lifted from my arms and into the air. Isabella snapped the finger in her right hand. A small ball of fire was hovering in the palm of her right hand. Slowly she put the Samantha doll over the flame. Samantha's body slowly caught on fire.

I screamed for her as her body burst into flames. Isabella laughed sadistically as Samantha screamed and cried. There was nothing I could do.

I watched in terror as Samantha's body slowly started deteriorating. As the doll's limbs fell and burned to ashes, so did Samantha's. After a few minutes of brutal torture there was nothing left of Samantha but scattered ashes. I sat there in shock, watching the specs of Samantha's remains float in the air.

I held my body in fear as I cried uncontrollably. Isabella just sat there laughing hysterically. But then there was this strong draft of the wind. I could hear Samantha's dark and haunting laugh.

Isabella stopped her laughing to watch. The ash remains of Samantha started shining red and were spiraling around us with the wind like a tornado. Isabella looked at the doll and became shocked. Its ash remains were forming together.

She said, "What's going on?" She tried to pick up

the doll but a strong gust of wind pushed her back. She sat on the ground and watched the doll slowly drag towards the vortex of ash. Samantha kept laughing as the ash started coming together. Slowly it started taking shape of a body.

"Tell me something, witch," Samantha said. Her face formed in the ash. "How can you kill what's already dead?" The ash glowed red as Samantha's body finally came back together. It was flawless. She held the voodoo doll in her hand and laughed.

Isabella got on her feet fast saying, "What...what are you? I incinerated you! Just what the hell are you?"

Samantha's voice had gotten darker. Her eyes were shining crimson. She started slowly walking towards Isabella after throwing away the voodoo doll.

She said, "You already know what I am. A fiend. A blood-sucking monster. One of the tainted. A cursed child of the night." She started running at Isabella as she laughed.

Isabella began backing up. She said, "Oh no." She lifted her hand to fire more magic. But Samantha quickly ran to her and grabbed her wrist.

She said, "How about an anatomy lesson, little witch. Can witches regenerate limbs like daywalkers can? Let's see."

Isabella pleaded for her to stop. But Samantha was ruthless. She jerked Isabella forward and gave her a heavy kick to the chest. Her arm ripped from her body as she flung back. Samantha stared at the limb in her hand.

She said, "Well. Guess not. Sorry about that." She tossed it and started walking towards Isabella.

Isabella screamed in agony as she kicked and rolled on the ground. She stopped when she realized Samantha was standing over her.

She grinned saying, "What's the matter, witch? I thought you said you'd have no problem killing a half-blood. It seems to me like you're having a lot of problems with killing me. I'm a cursed child, not a monster you fool!"

Samantha kicked her in the face. As Isabella flew further back, Samantha vanished and slammed her into the ground. She picked her up and punched her away. Isabella didn't stand a chance. Samantha was rag dolling her. When Isabella got up, Samantha would simply knock her back down repeatedly. She was being tortured.

Quickly I got up. "Stop. Samantha stop! That's enough!"

She didn't hear me. Her eyes got more and more

red as she continued thrashing Isabella. Rage or whatever it was inside of Samantha was taking control of her. She had gone berserk. She was keeping Isabella inches away from death on purpose, so she could torture her more and more. Before she could throw the last punch I grabbed her.

She looked back at me and roared like a wild animal. I felt the entire forest shake. She grabbed and pinned me down. She screamed over and over.

"Samantha snap out of it! It's me! Thomas! You have to calm down. Please." I held her face. She knocked my hand away and threw a fist at me. I moved out of the way as it dug into the dirt.

"SAMANTHA," I shouted. She had lost it. I was barely holding her back as she tried over and over to attack me. She grinned at me and I realized she was toying with me. With no effort at all she pinned me down and grinned. I could see her sharp fangs as she opened her mouth. She came so close.

"I'm not afraid of you," I said. "You're not a monster! You're not some freak or weirdo like they say! I've seen it. You're a good person. A beautiful person. Whatever this is don't let it control you Samantha! Fight it!"

Her teeth came close to my face. But she stopped as I spoke.

I said, "You're more than whatever this is.

You're kind. You just saved my life. I know you've been watching me. You knew she was a witch. You've been making sure I was safe. Samantha you're not a monster." She jerked away as she shut her eyes. She sat up and held her head as she screamed.

I said. "Fight it Samantha. Don't let this control you. You're beautiful, kind and gentle. You did what you had to do to protect me. You even gave her a chance to live." I took her face and kissed her. She tried pulling away but I held her close. Slowly her grip got lighter and lighter. I held her close in my arms.

When I pulled away her eyes had lost their bright red glow. They were just red. She was breathing hard and looking around as if she didn't know what happened.

She said, "Thomas." She gasped and stood "Where is Isabella?" She stopped when she saw Isabella's mangled body on the ground. She was barely alive.

Samantha held her head and said, "Oh no. I blacked out." She looked at me and grabbed me. She said, "Did I hurt you? Let me look at you."

I said, "No I'm fine, Samantha. You tried to attack me. But I think I managed to calm you down. Isabella burned you alive with her doll. You came back and went ballistic."

She said, "I'm so sorry. When I lose control of my anger the curse's hold on me strengthens. I black out and try to kill everything around me. Oh my gosh. This is why I wanted to stay away from you. I could have killed you!"

I said, "But you didn't! I brought you out of it. Samantha I don't want you to be away from me like this. I actually like you."

"Listen to yourself," she said. "You sound insane. You can't seriously want to be with a monster! I almost killed you."

"What have you done?" Someone shouted.

We looked back. A man with silver hair and a black robe was kneeling over Isabella. Behind him were dozens of people dressed in hooded robes.

Samantha said, "Witches and warlocks. Isabella's not alone."

The warlock held Isabella in his arms. "Sweetie? Sweetie wake up!"

A woman with red hair raced to him. She knelt down and took Isabella in her arms. She said, "She's still breathing. But barely alive. Have one of the healers give her treatment immediately."

She gave Isabella to the man and looked at Samantha.

The witch stood and said, "I take it you're the one who attacked my daughter. You're a long way from home aren't you night child? I thought your kind was forbidden to walk amongst the living."

Samantha put me behind her and said, "My situation is special. I have permission to be here under the condition that I never reveal myself to any humans."

The witch glanced at me and said, "Isn't that a human behind you?"

Samantha said, "Your daughter attacked him and performed dark magic on him. I came to his rescue. I don't want any trouble. Let us leave peacefully and..."

The man holding Isabella shouted. He said, "Leave peacefully? This fiend has nearly killed our daughter! There will be no peace here, daywalker. Not until we see your body in ashes."

"I agree," said the witch. "I will deal with her." She pulled out a black wand and stepped towards Samantha.

Samantha pushed me away saying, "Get away from here! Go."

I said, "I can't just leave you and I also have no clue where I am!"

"Both of you will die right here. Prepare yourselves." She raised her wand.

As quickly as she raised her wand it was quickly swooped away by something fast. Everyone looked around to see what it was. It landed in front of the witch. I couldn't see who it was because it was so dark. But it looked like a woman with long brown hair and large black wings coming from her back.

She said, "I came here because I sensed a lot of dark energy being thrown around. None of that stuff is allowed around the humans. It could cause a lot of disorder and mayhem. You all know that." She broke the wand in half and tossed it.

The witch said, "That daywalker behind you attacked my daughter! We came to her aide is all. You should be worried about her. She has a human with her!"

The woman looked at us. Samantha held on to me. She said, "Only because they're daughter attacked him. I came to save him from her. She was performing dark arts on him."

The witch shouted, "She's a liar! My daughter would never!"

As she started arguing, the winged woman let out a deafening scream. Everyone got silent as they covered their ears.

She said, "I'm not in charge of regulating monster laws. My job is to execute any supernatural threats to humans. That includes witches performing dark arts."

Isabella's father said, "You're going to take that leech's side? This is madness!"

She looked at the pentagram and said, "Those are clearly ritual markings." She held up the voodoo doll of Samantha. Its effect wasn't working anymore.

She said, "This is a body possession doll. One of my partners safely destroyed the human replica. So yes. Based on hard evidence I'm taking the leech's side. Seeing how the boy is fine I won't kill your already half-dead daughter. Take her home and get her treated."

The witches started to outrage. Isabella's mother said, That abomination nearly killed our daughter. Isabella is human. Do something about this!"

"Yeah! Tear her apart and burn her remains!" Another witch said.

Samantha grabbed me and said, "This is going to get bad. Step back."

"I am warning you all to leave at once!" The winged woman shouted. "I won't ask again!"

Isabella's father said, "Worthless bat. I'll kill her myself!"

He took out a wand and shot red bolts of lighting at the winged woman. Her wings wrapped around her body and repelled each strike. Suddenly I heard screams as more women with wings fell from the sky and attacked the witches. A war of claws and magic broke out right in front of me. Samantha held me down as lighting strikes shot all around the forest.

Samantha said, "We have to run while they're all

distracted! Thomas!" I felt dizzy and weak. Samantha kept shouting at me. But I couldn't keep my eyes open. Before I knew it, my body was falling towards the ground and everything was fading away.

6. Cursed Child

Everything had felt like a dream. Isabella being a psychotic witch. Samantha being a daywalker or whatever she said. Magic and monster brawls? No. It all had to be a dream. When I woke up in my room I was relieved. I sat up and let out a deep breath. My arm was completely fine and my body didn't have a single scratch on it.

Just to be safe I checked the date. I took my phone out. It read; **Monday, October 17th 2016**

I put my phone down and laughed loudly. It had all been a crazy dream. It was Monday morning and I hadn't gone to school yet. Everything had been a dream. Samantha watching me at school, the exam, talking to Caroline and Isabella drugging me and taking me out to a forest to perform sorcery on me. I laughed hard as I got out of the bed.

"Vampires and witches!" I held my stomach and laughed as I walked out of the bedroom. I called for my dad. "Hey! I had this crazy dream I want to tell you about. Dad?" I walked down a dim hallway. It was oddly longer and more narrow than usual. I didn't remember us having ten rooms on the first floor. I also didn't remember us having shelves and antiqued vases along the walls.

I stopped walking when it hit me. It wasn't *my* bed I had woken up in. But the smell from the bed was familiar. Sweet cherries. Quickly I grabbed my shirt and sniffed it. The scent was on it as well.

I raced downstairs and my thoughts were confirmed. I was in Samantha Black's house. But if it was still Monday that meant nothing in the dream happened. Samantha Black had kidnapped me somehow.

"I want to tell you a secret. Promise not to tell a soul. Or I might have to kill you."

I knew something was going to happen. My anxiety started racing as I looked around for her. She was nowhere to be seen. Quickly I raced for the front door. When I opened it I ran but tripped over someone. I toppled over onto the pavement. I held my face as it throbbed.

"You finally woke up. Good."

A shiver ran down my spine. I turned around and there she was. Samantha Black, sitting on the doorstep. She was holding a mirror as she held her face up with her free hand. She wasn't looking at me but into the mirror.

I said, "You can't keep me here. You have to let me go."

She said, "Go then. Who's stopping you?" She kept looking into the mirror.

I slowly stood and said, "Really? You're letting me go?"

She said, "You seem well enough to walk home. There's no reason for you to stay any longer."

I said, "Well enough? What are you talking about?"

She looked at me. I almost thought it wasn't a dream. But I saw her brown eyes. Again I let out a deep breath as I laughed. The redness wasn't there.

She said, "It wasn't a dream. I also haven't kidnapped you. I brought you here so you could heal."

I jumped back. I didn't want to believe it. Then I took out my phone and checked the date again. I laughed and said, "No. It's still Monday! None of that stuff..." I stopped when I realized Samantha couldn't possibly have known about my dream unless she either had the same one or it actually happened.

She said, "*Last* Monday Isabella Butler attempted to make you her slave. However I had been watching you since the night at the theater. I followed you two to the forest and waited for the right moment to save you.

"My curse took control over me and nearly made me kill you both. However you saved me. Then more witches came to Isabella's aid but was confronted by the Night-Hunters. A fight between the witches and night hunters broke out. You passed out, but I was there to get you away. I took you to my home, healed you and allowed you to stay until you recovered. That is what happened."

I stared at her trying to figure out what to say. I didn't want to believe any of it. But it had to be true. I stood there not knowing what her plans with me were. I already knew she was way faster than any human let alone me. Running was pointless.

She said, "I'm not going to hurt you. I promise. You can leave. Just don't say anything to anyone."

She never looked at me. She didn't sound angry either. If anything, Samantha sounded depressed. I turned away and started walking. That's when I felt her watching me. I stopped to meet her gaze.

I said, "You're just going to let me go? Just like that?"

She held her head down, looking back into the mirror. She said softly, "Yes. I have no choice. Please be safe. I can't keep saving you. I can't be near you. Last time I lost control and almost killed you. You saw what I am. Go home."

I stood there for a moment. Before, I was never able to read her. I could never tell if she was happy, sad or upset. She was always clear of emotion. But suddenly I could read her. Right then and there I could hear the sadness in her voice. I could read her sluggish body language. Samantha was depressed.

I walked back to her. I shrugged and said, "You can't expect me to just leave after you saved my life can you?" I sat with her.

She said, "I can't hold you prisoner can I?" She looked at me and smiled. But it was filled with doubt and grief.

I said, "No. Not a prisoner. Something better than that. I know you don't want me to stop seeing you. I never have. Not even now when I know that you're, well, you know."

She said softly, "Daywalker. I am a daywalker. A vampire of not only the night but also the day." She looked at the sun. "The sun won't burn my kind away. We're cursed to roam the Earth for an eternity. Suffering pain, bondage and loss over and over. I am unable to die."

I said, "And even though you're a daywalker, I choose to still be here. With you. I choose to be with you regardless. So stop pushing me away."

She snatched her hand away. She said, "Stop it. Don't be a fool. You would be in constant danger around me. I nearly killed you last week. I won't let that happen again."

She kept looking into the mirror. When I glanced

at it I noticed she was looking at me through it. But I couldn't see her reflection.

She said, "You see it now don't you? The mirror doesn't see me. Now you understand why they fear me. Why they torment me. Their hearts feel what their eyes can not see. I am monster, Thomas. A bloodsucking monster!"

She got up and threw her mirror against the pavement. Glass shards flew all over the ground as she stood there breathing hard.

She said, "I did everything I could think of to push you away. I ignored you. I was ice cold. I even left. Why did you push through my cold wall? Why did you ignore my warnings? You forced me to show this hideous form with your kind words and captivating aroma that tames my soul."

She sounded as if she was crying. But I never saw tears. When I stood she turned to me crying in a tearless rage.

She shouted, "What? Do you want to flee away like the others? Well go then! Run away from the demon girl, never to give her a glance again. Leave me to the loneliness and solitude that has befriended me for centuries now."

I felt so bad for her. I just stood there as she shouted at me with such obvious pain. So desperately she was hiding her sadness with coldness and anger. Underneath Samantha's quiet and calm exterior lied a scared, hurt and lonely little girl. She hid it so well.

She shouted, "Why haven't you ran away? Are you scared? Go! RUN!"

I shouted back, "I don't want to leave you! I never have!"

She stepped to me. I could see the red in her eyes. She shouted with a mix of anger and hurt, "What's your problem? Why don't you fear me like everything else does?"

She grabbed and pulled me fiercely to her face. She glared into my eyes. "Look into the red abysses of terror, Thomas. Your bones stiffen and the hairs on your skin rise when I'm near, don't they? Every nerve in your body is screaming, run."

I said, "Samantha, I'm not afraid of you. I care about you so much and just want to be closer to you. Stop crying." I wrapped my arms around her trying to let her know it was ok and that she was safe from any fear she thought I could ever have.

She said, "I don't understand. Why aren't you afraid? How can you look into these eye and not even flinch?"

I said, "I'm not running like the others. So if this is why you've been avoiding me then stop. I won't give up now. You saved my life and I know you have feelings for me."

She pushed away and said, "You should be afraid

of me! Call me a name and flee like the rest of them." Her guard finally dropped and her voice got softer. "None of them can stand me and it's because I'm this thing. I never asked for it to happen. Eventually you too will leave. Stop trying to be so different."

I said, "Samantha, I don't completely understand what you are. But I do know you've never hurt me and when I'm with you, things are so much better. You aren't like the others. I'm not being different. I'm being myself and you don't scare me. I'm not going to leave."

She looked back at me and said, "You're such an odd, boy! Foolish, odd, sweet, kind and..." She sniffed the air then cupped her face with her hands as she turned away, "...so captivating."

When I held her from behind, it startled her. But it didn't take her but a second to relax and hold me. This time there wasn't resistance and her body was calm.

She hesitated to speak, "If you mean what you say, perhaps we should go courting."
"Courting?"

She held me close and looked at me with her half shut, glimmering red eyes, "I believe they call it dating now. I am asking that you take me out."

I quickly took her hand and led her down the trail, before she had time to change her mind. Then

I realized my car was at my home. She laughed a little and put keys in my hand. She led me to her garage. As we got close it slowly opened and I saw a crimson colored Camero.

"Wow!" I ran inside and looked at it. It looked brand new and shiny red. The windows were tinted and the tires were clean. The paint job was flawless. On the hood were two black vertical stripes.

She said, "Do you mind driving? I've only driven once and I wreaked the last car. With being super fast I don't really need to learn how to drive. So I never did. You're probably better at it. Drive it whenever I suppose. Unless we breakup of course."

She started walking towards the passenger's side. I quickly ran to the door and opened it for her.

She smiled and said, "What a gentleman. Thank you." She sat inside and I closed the door.

The drive was silent for a while as we drove through the city. Samantha lived on the outskirts of the big city so it took a while to arrive. I didn't know what to say. She was a vampire. How was I supposed to ask about something like that? She had *just* let her guard down. Even though I had a lot of questions I decided not to ask.

I took us to the Demerra Theater. When I parked I saw her looking at me. She said, "You have questions. I don't mind them at all. You deserve to know what you're dealing with."

I said, "How do you know I wanted to ask questions?"

We got out of the car and started walking. She took my hand and pointed to a park a little ways away from the theater.

She said, "To be honest I'd enjoy a quiet walk or relaxing in the park more than a movie."

I nodded and led her to the park. There were tons of parents with their children. Some were on the jungle gym and slides while others were on the swings.

As soon as Samantha's foot touched the mulch everyone stopped to stare. As we walked towards the swings, the parents got their children and watched Samantha. Every single one of them gave her this look. They were looks of disgust, fear and nervousness. I realized it was the same look kids at our school gave her.

Samantha kept her eyes on the ground as she walked. She gave a little girl the slightest glance. Her mother quickly grabbed her and led her away from the playground. When her and I sat on the swings, everyone was gone. Samantha dropped her shoulders as if defeated and watched the ground.

"It's just us now," she said softly. "I'm sorry. I can't really help it."

I said, "Is it like that with everyone? They just stare and walk away?" Her eyes glimmered red when she looked at me. I had to be close to see the redness of her irises. If I was but a few feet away they seemed brown.

She said, "Everyone except you. You're the first living person to stay this close in over two centuries. They flee because of the vibration my energy throws out. It either makes them nervous or afraid. It's the curse. There is nothing I can do to control it. Even when I sit alone and remain quiet they watch and fear me."

I said, "I don't feel anything like that when I'm around you. It made me nervous when you said you might kill me. But that's it. Two centuries?"

She nodded. "I was turned on my 18th birthday. Over two hundred years ago, February the 7th. If you're wondering why I look this young, it's because my aging stopped when I was 20."

"Wow," I said. "That's so cool. I can only imagine all of the things you've gotten to see. Two hundred years and you don't even age. Samantha what's it like being a vampire? I mean besides the stares. What all can you do?"

She said, "Since I was turned my strength, senses and speed have gone far past human levels. Something unique though are my eyes. One glance and I can charm, scare or even seduce anyone." She looked at me. "Well not *anyone*. They don't work on you for some reason."

I said, "Samantha that's so amazing. That's why Caroline freaks out every time you look at her. The day she fought you. She was so terrified because of your eyes."

She smiled deviously and laughed. She said, "Yes. Also I can hear the thoughts of others. It's not mind reading though. I can't control the thoughts I hear. It's like being around people when they talk. You don't choose to listen. Your ears pick up the noise. My mind picks up thoughts."

I'm sure my mouth was opened. The more she talked the more incredible I thought she was. She was like some medieval super woman. But a bit darker. It was like some dark fairytale. And somehow I was lucky enough to be so close to her. She had even saved my life more than once.

I said, "You could totally help me pass my exams."

She sat on a swing laughing, "That's the first thing you say? You're amusing."

"Scoot over, Samantha."

She looked at me as I stood from my swing. I could tell by the look in her eyes. She couldn't believe I wanted to be so close. But it got her to turn away as she tried to hide her beautiful smile.

I sat with her. Then I held her in my arms. Her body was cold as ice. Just like her kisses. She knew I had noticed and gave me a glance.

"Sorry," she said.

I touched her face. I said, "You're freezing."

"You're burning," she said as she rubbed my arm. I held my palm against hers and hers against mine. There was this mix of cold and warm. It created this balanced sensation of hot and cool. Our hands eventually interlocked. My hand kept hers warm while hers kept mine cool. We were like two halves of a whole.

I said, "Wow. The stories are true. Cold and pale skin. So do you, I mean, you know."

She looked at the night sky. When the moon hit her eyes, they shined red. When she opened her mouth to speak, I saw her sharp fangs.

"*Blood* sucker," she said. "Yes. I drink blood. Without blood I become weak and my body eventually shuts down. It became instinctual after the curse took me. If I go too long without blood, I become frail and weary. It's like my air. I need it to breathe. Thomas…" She sniffed the air and looked my way.

I said, "Is that what you mean when you say you can't help yourself around me?"

"More than I realized," she said. "Thomas last week when you held me, some of your blood dripped onto me. During my fight with Isabella. And I think it's part of the reason I frenzied so badly. When I tasted it, I got this powerful surge of power rushing through me. It was incredible…"

She looked at me.

"But it also made me lose control. Thomas you are a possible trigger. What we're doing is very dangerous."

I held her. I said, "Yes. I know. But I also stopped you. I brought you out of your rampage. I think that means something. I helped you control your curse. I'm also not afraid of you. If this really was dangerous, I'd be dead right now."

I couldn't help myself around her. We were having this serious conversation. The next thing I knew I was caressing her arms and moving in for a kiss. She held my face and pressed her lips against mine. I felt her body get tense as she tightened her grip. She turned away.

She said, "Your aroma. It's too satisfying. I can hardly stop myself from biting you. One sip and I'll lose myself again."

I kissed her face. Then her neck. She let out a heavy sigh and went limp. I held her in my arms and looked at her. She was dazed.

She said, "How can you make me so wild yet tame all at once? This is dangerous, Thomas. What will you do if I lose control? Are you really willing to risk your life for a filthy leech?"

I pulled her close and kissed her. I said, "Don't call yourself that. I just have to teach you how to control yourself. I can't help myself around you either, Samantha."

"Teach me to control myself?"

I nodded. "Go slow and relax your mind," I said.

I softly put my mouth against hers. Immediately her breathing sped up as her muscles twitched and she grabbed me. I held her back gently as she tried to kiss me again.

I laughed. "You're anxious. Go slow and stay relaxed. Don't lose control."

She was getting frustrated with herself. She got up and kicked some mulch up.

She said, "I'm hopeless. I'm not used to this. It's been over two hundred years since I was with someone who was alive. It's hard to relax when you have such a sweet-smelling scent."

I walked to her and touched her arm. She watched me as I rubbed her face. She cupped my hands on her face and nestled in them, taking their warmth.

I said, "Don't be so hard on yourself. We'll work on it. Just mirror what I do."

I kissed her. She began breathing hard again as her body tensed up again. "Slow and easy," I said in-between a kiss. Slowly she became less stiffened and more relaxed. Still, she was a little strong but I could tell she was gaining control.

She pulled away. She said, "I want to try again.

Thomas I think that I'm learning how to kiss you without crushing you. Let's try it once more."

It made me laugh. "I never said stop in the first place."

She batted her eyes and quickly leaned in. She stopped when her face was inches away. Slowly and gently, she pressed her lips against mine. She was learning how to tame herself fast. This time she was holding me lightly and her kisses were soft.

I pulled away. She panicked and said, "I tried my best! Oh no. Did I hurt you?"

I shook my head. "No. You were perfect. You..."

Gently she swatted my hand away and kissed me as she wrapped her arms around me. I did the same. Her kisses were cold and sensational. Each time she stopped to breathe her cold and sweet breath teased my lips as I anticipated the spark from the first, making my heart thunder as she held her soft body against mine. Our breaths intertwined as our lips said hello in a soft moist dance.

She stopped, but didn't let me go. Her ruby red eyes were now staring into mine. Under the moonlight they seemed to glisten. For a moment, she looked away towards the parking lot as if watching someone.

"Hey," I said. She looked at me as I said, "Are you ready to leave?"

"Only if it's with you," she said.

I smiled, "What makes you think I was going to leave any other way?" Our fingers laced and I began walking back to the car with Samantha Black.

7. Knight from the Sky

The month of October seemed to pass fast. It was coming to its end and winter had slowly made itself known. Since the night I found out she was a daywalker, I had started spending more and more time with Samantha Black. Eventually she dropped her guard around me and there wasn't any distance between us at all.

Samantha was from a province called, Nightingale. She told me about a secret society separate from the humans. Supernatural creatures like vampires roamed there freely without persecution. It was their sanctuary. It was located somewhere near Ukraine. It explained why she had such a thick and exotic accent.

It was easy to lose track of both the time and people around us when I was with her. A lot of the time we would sit together somewhere around the school. Sometimes we would sit outside and just watch the sunset. Things were really simple with her. All we ever did was laugh and talk. We weren't a boring couple though. We did go out on dates.

At first it was hard to watch how people acted around her. We would go somewhere like a restaurant or a movie theater. More and more people would leave the longer we stayed. If we decided to stay long only the staff would stick around. But Samantha never frowned and always laughed when I was with her. I think I made her reality more bearable. She wasn't alone anymore.

One of our favorite spots to hangout at was outside of the school. We would sit on either the bleachers on the football field or one of the benches anywhere around the school. Samantha loved to gaze the sky and the football field.

She said she loved how nature was always so calm and unbothered. It also didn't flee from her. It made her feel *there*. With people always running from her, it made her feel like she was a ghost. But nature made her feel normal. It made me happy to see her smile. So I didn't mind watching the sky with her. I loved the simplicity of things.

We sat on the bleachers one Friday after school had ended. The football players and cheer squad were practicing. Samantha and I sat towards the very top by ourselves as usual. She had this really unique gift.

I looked amongst the crowds of students gathering around the school buses. They were all behind us near the school entrance. There was this couple arguing.

I pointed and said, "Ok, Samantha. How about them?"

She looked back and saw them. She tilted her left ear towards them.

She smiled and said, "Her boyfriend has dirty photos of his teacher on his phone. He's making up a pretty weak excuse. He says that he has no idea how they got there. But the truth is, he's a pervert."

"Wow," I said. "Samantha that's incredible. How'd you figure out that last part?"

She winked. "I heard his thoughts. When I first got this curse I could hear all of the thoughts of the people around me. At first it was overwhelming. But I learned how to tune them out and focus on certain ones. It's pretty useful at times."

I leaned away saying, "What am I thinking now?"

She grabbed me by the shirt with one hand. When she pulled me in she kissed me saying, "Look who's found us."

She motioned in front of us. Martinez and Ace were halfway up the bleachers. Samantha had no problem with who saw us together and when. In fact she always made it clear *she* was with me. I liked it. She sat on my lap and held me.

She said, "They can't believe you're with the weird and quiet girl and that you spend more time with her than with them. The bigger one misses you as his lab partner."

I said, "You aren't weird and they're going to have to get used to me dating you. Samantha I want to ask something. Your eyes look brown again. What makes them change?"

She looked towards the sun and brushed her bangs out of her eyes.

"Look closer," she said. As the sun hit her face her eyes turned dark red. It was barely noticeable.

She said, "The sun has to hit them at the right angle. I keep my bangs long so normal humans don't notice my actual eye color. I also haven't had anything to drink lately." She turned away.

"Blood," I said.

She nodded. "If I have enough, my eyes and hair are more visibly red. At night, the redness in my eyes no longer hide. They glow under moonlight. When I drink blood the shine gets brighter. If you can't see my eye color at night, I'm due for a feeding."

I said, "But they haven't been glowing for a couple of days now."

She nodded. "I know. I've gone without for a while."

"I don't get it. Your eyes had a glow during the

day just a few days ago."

She laughed and bit her finger. She turned away saying, "That's because the last time I had blood it was a rare type..." She looked at me and said, "You have no clue do you? Thomas the last thing I had blood from is you?"

"Me?" I said in confusion. I touched my face and neck, but couldn't find any marks or cuts.

I said, "When? I don't remember it."

She said, "During my fight with Isabella. Do you remember how you held me in your arms when she cut my throat open? You had cuts all over your body. Including your face. A very, very small drip fell on my lip."

I was so caught in the moment of thinking she was dying that I didn't think about it. The blood from my cuts dripped onto her face and mouth. That's when she opened her eyes and smiled.

Samantha continued, "That very small amount was unlike anything I have ever had. It lasted me for nearly a month. Animal blood usually lasts me a couple of weeks. Human blood is supposed to be very potent. But your blood..."

She looked at me.

"Your blood did more than feed me. It made me stronger, faster and my senses were even more incredible than they are now. I even healed faster. Thomas your blood made me invincible. I believe you have a rare blood type us vampires call, Super Sânge. It's thought to be only a myth. But you're proof of its existence. You're one in a million."

"Wow," I said. "So I'm like your drug."

"More like my kryptonite. Thomas I believe your blood is the reason I frenzied so badly. The power surge was so great and it fueled my anger towards Isabella. Super sânge's incredible effects come with a price. I lose absolute control and go rampant. I can never do that again."

I held her close and kissed her.

I said, "You worry too much. You're forgetting that I calmed you down. I also taught you how to kiss me without crushing me. Ms. Black, we make the perfect team."

She laughed as I pulled her in and started pecking her neck repeatedly with my lips. When I did that she would always wrestle me and of course, with her superhuman strength I never won (unless she let me). Eventually she'd get me in her arms and nestle her cheek against my neck, slowly and gently nibbling and kissing on my face.

I held her head saying, "I will never get over how good this feels."

She giggled. "Me neither. It's hard not the bite you. Would you be mad if I did? Just a little pinch?"

"Ugh! You two are at it again?" It was Martinez. Samantha and I looked up and saw him and Ace standing in front of us.

Samantha held me and said, "Sorry gentlemen. I can't help myself when he's so close. You should have him give you girl advice."

"Yeah because I want to date the kind of girls he attracts," Martinez sassed. He couldn't have been more sarcastic if he tried.

He said, "You two seriously need to get a room. For crying out loud, there's people watching you." He pointed to our left. It was a girl I had never seen before. Samantha rubbed her face against mine.

She said, "Who says we don't already have a room? Maybe we're warming up for the private things." She giggled.

Ace and Martinez groaned and nearly gagged.

Martinez said, "Keep that stuff to yourself. Thomas I know you've been busy with *it* but today is the night of the Halloween party. Are you coming?"

"Please!" Ace said. "It's only once a year and you never hangout with us anymore!"

"Hmm. A Halloween party sounds interesting," Samantha said.

"You won't even have to dress up, Samantha," Martinez laughed.

Before I could bark at him she said, "Good point. This is the one night where I don't have to hide who I am. What do you think?"

Martinez said, "Thomas come on. Besides, maybe you could find someone normal. Thomas?"

I was looking at the girl he had pointed out earlier. She had long and wavy brown hair and brown skin. Now that I had gotten a chance to see her, I realized she looked familiar. I had been seeing her more and more around the school lately. Usually she was with friends but this time she was alone.

"Earth to Thomas!" Martinez said. He knocked on my head.

I swatted his hand away saying, "Cut that out! Sure I'll go. But I'm bringing Samantha so be nice to her. And don't pull any stunts." Like egging her, tarring her in feathers or some weird high school prank like that. It was for their safety not hers. I would hate to see what Samantha would do if they pissed her off beyond her control.

She held me and said, "Yes. Him and I will attend this lovely party. Thank you for the invite, Martin."

"Martinez! Stop calling me, Martin!"

Samantha laughed as she apologized. I couldn't join her because I was trying to figure out who that girl was. It felt like she was watching us. But, why? I watched as she waved at me casually. She kept drawing in her black pad. A witch? Isabella hadn't returned to school since Samantha nearly killed her.

The entourage of warlocks and witches that saved her made me wonder if someone had their eye on Samantha, the daywalker.

She kept her eye on me while she kept sketching. She waved again but, this time she smiled flirtatiously. I looked away fast to Samantha and my friends. Martinez and Samantha were going back and forth with insults. When I looked back at the girl she was still watching. She didn't even care that I noticed.

Suddenly Samantha got up. I missed what had happened. She said, "Thomas I need to excuse myself."

I said, "Huh? Why?"

Martinez laughed, "What's the matter?"

She glared at him saying, "You mean you aren't happy that the *freak* is finally leaving?" She starting talking the way Martinez did. Her voice got lower and somewhat annoying (like Martinez).

She said, *"Why is Thomas hanging out with that gothic weirdo? Why is the freak here?"*

Martinez gasped. He said, "What? How are you... I never said those things out loud."

She went on, *"Ace and I should find him a date and fast. Or he'll end up missing or worse."* She kept going. Martinez started freaking out. He demanded to know how she was doing that. Doing what? I didn't understand what he meant.

Then I finally realized what was going on. She was invading his mind. She must have heard him think those things and got hurt. Now she was throwing his hurtful thoughts back at him. Making him a prisoner in his own mind.

I had to pull her away. She wasn't going to stop until she felt he was just as hurt as she was. Martinez didn't say a word. He was too busy covering his ears as he begged her to stop. I took her by the hand and led her down the bleachers.

She said, "Thomas let me go. I'm fine. Please. I'm sorry."

When we got to my car I finally did. I sat on the hood and watched her. She looked away as if she knew the talk was coming. She rolled her eyes and shook her head.

I said, "You heard the rude things he was thinking didn't you? I'm sorry. He's a jerk. But you can't do what you just did back there. You have to control yourself. Not just with me but everyone around you."

She said, "I know. I shouldn't have done that. But it's not like anyone would believe him anyway. He got what he deserved." She sat beside me on the car and held me.

I said, "Samantha no one can find out what you are. Not a single person. If you raise a lot of suspicion then people will snoop. My friends and especially Caroline. You can't draw too much attention or someone will find out so…"

"Fine!" She shouted. "I'll keep to myself and be silent like before. Who cares? They all hate me and I can't do a damned thing about it. Why fight back? I can smile, I can compliment them, hell I could be the sweetest woman ever and they would all still HATE me!"

She slammed her fist on the hood of my car. She nearly hit me but I never flinched. I watched as she dug her fist from the large dent she made. Her breathing sped up and she kept clenching and unclenching her fists. Her claws slowly started to show and I could see her fangs when she opened her mouth.

She muttered, "Why did this have to happen to me? What sin did I commit to deserve this dark and lonely curse? Do you know what it's like to be hated and feared by everyone around you? To hear every rotten and evil thing they think about you? Over 200 years have passed. Do you know what it's like to go through this for a whole century? This is my Hell. My eternity of damnation. There is no salvation for a fiend like me."

I said, "Stop it!" I pulled her close by her wrists. "Stop talking about yourself like that. You aren't a fiend!"

She pulled away and pointed to her face. I could

131

see the faint redness in her eyes and the sharp teeth in her mouth.

She said, "Open your eyes! I AM a fiend. Every living thing but *you* can see it. Look around us. It's like a ghost town. We're at the school for crying out loud. They avoid me. They flee! Absolute strangers fear me even when they don't know my dark truth.

"Samantha Black, the bloodsucking monster. Everything that I am sickens me. I hate my own flesh. It isn't as easy as you think. I can't just ignore my reality. It's not fair and I never asked for this."

She stood in front of me and watched the skies sadly. It was like she was wishing or looking for something. I looked around us and it was just like she said. No one was there. The parking lot was empty.

People would always walk a couple of yards away from her or around if possible. On the sidewalks my side of the pavement would be cluttered with people. But on Samantha's side she was always alone. Why couldn't they see the beauty that I was so lucky to discover?

After a long moment of silence I put my hand over hers. Her claws were still out and she was cold but I didn't care. I took her hand in mine and rubbed it to make it warm.

I said, "Samantha. Is it a terrible thing if I'm happy you're not human anymore?"

She scoffed a little. "Is that your idea of a joke? Sorry if I don't entertain it with a giggle."

"It's not a joke," I said. "If you hadn't become a vampire then you would have died long before I was born. I wouldn't be here right now. Well I would but not with you. I think that would suck."

She said, "It wouldn't matter. My worthless life makes no difference to yours."

I said, "You're wrong. You saved me from Isabella. No one else would have been able to. I would be her mind slave right now if you hadn't saved me. Before that you saved me from drowning. You said it yourself. I would have died."

She looked at me. "Are you forgetting how I blacked out and nearly killed you?"

I looked at the sky. She repeated her question but I ignored her. She got close to my face and followed my line of sight. She shook her head.

She said, "I don't understand. What are you staring at?"

I said, "You watch the sky a lot. You have rare eyes. It's like you can see things no one else can. Do you believe in angels?"

"Like God and Heaven?" She asked. "A century ago I gave up on the idea out of hatred. I couldn't figure out why something like this would happen to a little girl. What God would allow that?"

"But I've seen a lot of unexplainable acts of love

and miracles. God and his angels. Yes they exist. He just doesn't want a thing to do with me. He condemned me a while ago."

I gasped and quickly looked at her. She had her knees up. She was holding them with her head down, staring into the distance. Finally she realized the silence.

She said, "You don't agree? You think some higher being is out there who actually cares about me?"

"Yes," I said without hesitating. She looked at me as I went on. I said, "I think maybe it was your destiny to become cursed and that it was my destiny to meet you. We saved eachother. Without you, Isabella still would have existed and she still would have fell for me. You make a difference. I believe in angels. I'm looking at one."

She burst out laughing. Not her dark laugh but her happy laugh. It was the kind of laugh someone did when they were having a really good time. She held her chest as she tried to stop. Inevitably she kept laughing. It was hard not to smile whenever I heard it.

"Quite the charmer you are," she said. She crawled onto my lap and said, "But I'm no angel. I wish. But that's just not my..."

I stopped her with a kiss. The wintery sensations her lips gave mine had become addicting.

Sometimes I just wanted to shut her up and kissed her. She *was* an angel. My angel. I pulled away gently. Her eyes were half shut and she had become dazed again.

She smiled lightly, "How do you make me so wild yet tamed all at once?"

I said, "Forget about all of the mean things they think. You're no fiend. You're my fallen angel. Come on. Let's go down the rabbit hole and leave this boring world my, beautiful red dove."

I got off of the car and held my hand out. She took it and stood. She giggled and said, "And where will this rabbit hole take me?"

"Tonight I'm going to show you a really good time. We're going to that party and we're dancing the night away. Let's go get ready."

Samantha loved the idea of me taking her to a party. It was mostly because she liked to dance. We were going to get ready at her house. But she persisted on seeing my home. It was going to be her first time there. When we arrived she didn't wait for me to park along the curb. She had a habit of getting out the car before we stopped to park. Each time she did it, the car would jerk as if it hit some large bump in the road.

My neighborhood was nothing out of the ordinary. Mostly old people lived there so it was always quiet. Everyone always kept their lawn nicely cut and clean. Every car in their driveway was always spotless. The houses went from small to large and they all looked as if they were just painted. Somehow Samantha knew which one was mine. She stepped onto the sidewalk and stared.

17771 Hilt Avenue was engraved on the pink spotted mailbox she stood by. I watched her fingers crawl along the red flag sticking upward. Her eyes stared at the quiet and subtle home. It wasn't too big or too small. A standard home built for maybe four or five. It was painted white with a black rooftop like most of the other homes. A few windows were on each floor.

"Wow," she said as her feet planted onto the lawn. "It's beautiful. You live here." She said it like she had known for a while.

We walked on the lawn towards the front door. She savored each moment, taking each second to admire everything around her. First the empty but impressive driveway covered in flawless and grey cement. Then the four-meter sized oak tree in the middle of the lawn. Lastly the mat with an angel wings design in front of the door.

"This is amazing," she said.

I laughed a little. It was like she thought it was a palace or something.

I said, "Yeah but we aren't lucky enough to have a security system like you. Come on." I opened the door and went inside. Samantha stood outside in front of the mat. She hadn't taken a single step. She was waiting for me to invite her inside.

I shook my head. "It's fine. Come inside."

She took one step onto the mat then another into my home. Slowly she peeped her head in. Her eyes got even wider as her mouth gapped slightly. We were inside the dining room. It was a wooden floor covered room connecting to four areas: the kitchen, upstairs, the basement and the living room.

The dining room wasn't a typical one. It had no eating table and was mostly for show. There were family portraits all over the room, along with shelves with vases on them, mostly along the walls. The stairs leading to the bedrooms and the basement was directly ahead after coming into my house.

The living room was to the left. The kitchen was on the right. Everything was always clean and the house was always at an oddly perfect temperature. It was never hot or cold.

Samantha couldn't keep her eyes off of the chandelier hanging from the ceiling. She smiled and said, "It's lovely here. Whom do you live with?"

"I live with my father mostly. My sister, Marie is off at college. Sometimes she visits," I said.

She walked to a vase on a shelf. It was in front of a family portrait. She placed a single finger on it as she stared at the portrait. I could tell she was staring at my mother.

"And her?" She looked back at me. "This is your mother. What about her?"

I got beside her and joined her gaze.

I said, "She left one night when I was three or four. I'll never forget it. I thought it was some dream. She came to me in my sleep and told me she had to leave. She hugged me tight, kissed me and promised to come back. The next morning she really was gone. I haven't seen her since."

She softly said, "Oh. I'm sorry. I didn't know."

I said, "She abandoned us. No one knows why she left. No one can find her. This isn't a big deal, Samantha. It's just one of those things."

She said, "It must have hurt you a lot. Being left at such an early age. You felt discarded."

I didn't know if she was hearing my thoughts or if it was that easy to see how I felt. I didn't bother saying anything because she was right. She looked my way and smiled.

She said, "I don't know her so I can't speak against her. But I promise to never leave you. Now that you know what I am, I also promise to protect you no matter what. Even from the monster inside of me. For you, I will learn to control her. So open up. Don't be afraid to show how you feel around me."

For the first time in a long time I had felt *with*

someone. Whenever I was around my friends or at school I felt disconnected. I felt like I was there but in limbo. Just watching and observing everyone around me. Waiting for someone to connect. Emotionally alone.

Caroline was the only person who eased that feeling. When my mom left I met her a month later. Thinking about it made me realize she was my first friend. Caroline helped ease the pain of loss. Samantha Black was doing the same thing but it felt incredibly different. It felt unlimited.

She took my hands and got close. Before she could kiss me, she looked at the door. After a few seconds, the bolts on the lock rattled and it opened. It was my father and to my surprise, Marie. She hadn't changed at all. Her skin was still tan and her hair was still shoulder length and brown. I hugged her on sight.

I said, "You're home! Wow I wasn't expecting to see you until Thanksgiving."

Marie said, "I'm here for fall break. Dad insisted. I almost said no but he promised angel pie for dessert."

He was behind her laughing. He said, "It'll be nice to have a family dinner. I don't mind making the pie for dessert."

Marie turned and looked passed me. She said, "Caroline I love the new look! You dyed your hair.

You look a bit paler too."

Samantha was right behind me watching in this curious sort of way. She looked somewhat nervous and made no eye contact. It hit me that she was trying her best not to make them nervous or scared.

I said, "Oh, sorry! No you guys, this is Samantha Black. She moved here a couple of months ago. She's my new girlfriend."

She kindly bowed with her hands together. She said, "I'm pleased to meet you." They greeted her with excitement. Marie couldn't keep her eyes off of Samantha's hair.

She said, "Wow it's so glossy and healthy. What dye do you use?"

"All natural," Samantha said. She flipped it behind her shoulders. "All I use is shampoo and water."

They loved her. Not once did they flinch when Samantha's eyes met theirs. It was obvious she was surprised. She wasn't used to people *not* fearing her. She was still getting used to me not running away. Always wondering when I would leave or fear her. Now my family was smiling with her, laughing and hugging her.

It was nice to see. On a daily basis I watched people stare at her and avoid her. For once I wasn't the only person fascinated by her presence. She met more people who could see how great she was. It was so amazing that I forgot what she wasn't. Human. As my father shook her hand he noticed the chilling sensation her touch gave off.

He said, "Wow are you cold, Samantha? Your hand."

She gently pulled it away. She looked away saying, "Oh. No I just get cold easily. It's fine."

I said, "Well Samantha and I should hurry. We're going to a Halloween party tonight with my friends."

I slowly led her towards the stairs as they greeted her one last time. They even invited her to have dinner sometime. She kept staring at her hand and rubbing it with the other.

My home only had three levels: the main floor, upstairs and the basement. Up the staircase led to a long and narrow hallway. It was painted white with colorful wallpaper of flowers and navy blue carpeting. It had six rooms with three on each side. My room was the last one on the left. I let Samantha walk in first.

She was still watching her hand and rubbing it. I walked to her and asked if she was ok. It surprised me when I saw her smiling. She looked at me as her eyes glimmered. She was overjoyed.

She stuttered a little. She said, "They like me. They really like *me*! They didn't scream or run. They didn't even think anything rotten about me. Your family likes me."

She wrapped her arms around me. She was so happy that the hug nearly crushed me. But it didn't bother me. Seeing her so happy made me happy too.

She said, "I haven't felt this way in a long time. How can they not fear me? My dark energy should have suffocated them. I still don't know how *you're* immune to the effects of my curse."

I said, "You worry too much. Let's get ready for the party." After I kissed her I walked to the bathroom.

It only took a few minutes. The party was short notice. But I had a few costumes. Tylor liked to make short films. I always helped. So inevitably he had given me a few costumes. I decided to go to the party as a red Martian.

It was the typical egg headed alien costume. It had giant and black oval shaped eyes and antennas on its head. Instead of green it was red and its space suit was sparkling grey.

When I walked out of the restroom I saw Samantha sitting on my bed. She turned to me and shuddered back a little. "Wow. It's not easy to scare me. Are you an alien?"

I took off the mask and said, "Yup. What about you? You haven't even changed clothing."

She dug into her pocket and laughed a little. "You take five minutes. I take five seconds." She took out a small vial with what I assumed to be blood inside. She took off the cap and drunk the whole thing. I wasn't shocked or repulsed. Though I probably should have been.

When she was finished, her eyes closed and she tilted her head back. She let out a deep and satisfying breath. Her fangs and claws came out and her body started glowing a faint light red color. Slowly she looked at me and I could see the intense red glow of her eyes and hair. She seemed *different.* Not just with the way she looked but her attitude. She had a stronger presence and her strong confidence seemed even more intense.

She elegantly rose from the bed. No sooner when she stood, she disappeared. Black smoke appeared by the bed as I heard her behind me. Her arms were around my shoulders and her lips were closer to my ear. She laughed and said, "Just like that and your queen is ready. I will barely blend."

I said, "Is this what blood does to you?"

She laughed again. She said, "I'm quite the same. The blood just gives me a little rush. I feel more alive. I promise I'm safe to be around." She vanished and appeared in front of me. "I promise to be good. Just as long as no one lays a hand on you, my love."

She put her hand on my neck and came close with her mouth open. Her fangs came inches away from my lips. She smiled with her eyes shut just as her fangs shrunk. Slowly she kissed me. She had complete control over herself.

She whispered in my ear, "But if anyone hurts you in anyway, I will literally rip their throats out."

I carefully put her in front of me. She had the same grin she had the night she fought Isabella. It was full of bloodlust and poise. Anything that threatened her or me was in serious trouble. When Samantha had blood in her it was like her personality changed. A darker and less tamed version of herself surfaced.

She took my hand and said, "Relax. I promise. I promise not to hurt anyone and that I will be a good girl. Please don't stare at me like that. I won't hurt anyone. I promise."

The last time Samantha had a drop of blood in her, she blacked out. She nearly killed Isabella ruthlessly and she attacked me. Now she had more than a drop. This darker Samantha was hard to trust. It was only my second time meeting her. If anything made her angry there was no way of knowing if she would black out again and rampage. If she blacked out at a party filled with people it would be a complete nightmare.

She squeezed my hands softly and urged me to

trust her. She did black out. But I also managed to tame her darker side. Part of me believed Samantha was meant to be there with me and I was meant to be there with her. I had the ability to help her beat a side of her even *she* feared. I refused to be afraid and I refused to turn away from her.

She held my hands and urged again. She said, "I promise. Please trust me. No one gets hurt unless someone like Isabella comes. If someone tries something like that I won't hesitate to protect you. But I do have enough sense not to attack an ordinary human! Trust me. Please."

I said, "There's a chance they might try to pull a prank on you. The students might harass you and…"

She said, "I don't care about them! I care about you. Besides look at me, darling." She stepped back and flipped her hair back with a devious smirk. Her eyes shined as the moonlight hit them.

She said, "No one in their right mind would mess with me. I make their hearts rattle. We'll have the whole dance floor to ourselves."

I had to give her a chance. I didn't want to be another person who feared Samantha. I loved the way it made her smile when people around her loved her presence. I couldn't treat her like the average person would.

By some miracle I was one of the few people

who didn't fear her and I was drawn to her. I could help her control her inner monster. So I made it my duty to be by her side no matter what. I was going to take the dark Samantha out to dance.

The Halloween party was held at a huge building downtown. It was a large five-story building. The first floor looked like an old post office. The flooring was made of old marble and it was connected to a restaurant. We took the elevator to the fourth floor. As soon as the elevator door slid open we saw dozens of students dressed in costumes.

As soon as Samantha stepped out of the elevator everyone stopped to stare. She smiled, took my hand and led me through the long aisles everyone made for us. Strangely no one fled or walked away.

"Wow, she's beautiful."

"Awesome outfit."

"Her eyes are stunning."

They all couldn't keep their eyes off of her. We made our way by a mini-bar and stepped onto a large and round dance floor made of smooth wood. The lighting was dim and made everything seem really relaxed and peaceful. It was my first dance with Samantha Black. We danced right in the middle like she predicted.

Even though there were other students around, it felt like it was just her and I. She placed my hands on her waist and put her arms over my shoulders. I kept looking around waiting for everyone to disappear. But they were astonished by her presence. Not afraid. Samantha was like some goddess to be admired.

She said, "They won't go anywhere. I can tell by hearing what they're thinking."

I said, "But how? I thought your energy made them afraid."

She shrugged. "Good luck I guess. Let's just dance before they gain their senses."

We danced for several minutes. It felt like seconds. Samantha was literally glimmering under the dim lighting. Her darker side seemed way more confident and aloof.

We were getting stares but it was like she didn't notice. She laughed and smiled as we danced all around the room. Fast songs. Slow songs. It didn't matter. She adapted while staying elegant and beautiful.

As we danced I twirled her. She spun backward and as I caught her someone cut in between us. She grabbed my shoulders and looked deeply into my eyes. They were an odd ocean blue color.

She said, "Your girlfriend is really pretty. But not prettier than me huh, alien boy?"

"What?" It wasn't Isabella. Her skin was a honey brown color and her voice was softer. The white mask and dress sealed her identity. Somehow she seemed really familiar but I couldn't figure out why. She said, "I've seen you around. With her. I'm so jealous."

"What?" I gasped. When I pulled away she held me close.

She said, "Nice mask. But I can still tell it's you, Thomas Rouges. I've see you with your girlfriend around school. Is she supposed to be a vampire?"

I choked as soon as she said vampire. I coughed and tried to catch my breath.

She laughed. "For Halloween of course. Everyone knows they don't exist. Right?"

I laughed back. "Yeah. I thought you were crazy for a minute there."

She showed me the cross around her necklace. She smiled and said, "In the fictional world, I'd be your girlfriend's worst nightmare. I'm a demon hunter. Look at my cross. Like it?"

Before I could answer, Samantha returned. She grabbed the girl by the shoulder and turned her around. She said, "He's with me. Go dance somewhere else before you get hurt."

As soon as Samantha shot her a glare, the mysterious girl got nervous and backed away. She said, "Oh. I'm really sorry, Samantha. Please don't be upset. I couldn't resist."

"Just get out of here," Samantha said with a

laugh. She shooed her away and came back to me.

"Christine what are you doing?"

Samantha and I looked back. It was another girl. Her hair was black, curly and close to her lower back. There was a mask on her face too. Christine looked back at her and waved. Before walking away she gave me a wink through her mask.

Samantha smirked and said, "Stay far away, miss. He's with me."

Samantha and I stopped dancing for a while to have drinks and food. Non-alcoholic drinks of course. The party was being hosted by one of the students and there were parents around. We sat with my friends Tylor, Ace, Martinez and Williams. They all had dates of course. Except for Williams. I felt bad for him.

Martinez laughed as he held his date. She was a short redhead. Not the best looker but Martinez wasn't complaining. He said, "So your date *is* here, Williams? Where?"

He said, "She's somewhere around here. I wouldn't lie."

"Sure, sure. Wow, Samantha. You somehow look less creepier than usual," Martinez said.

She sighed as she took a drink. "Your dim witted jokes make me cringe. Read a book on insults or something."

We all laughed at her comeback. As we ate I saw

her stare off into space more and more. She seemed distracted. I asked her what was wrong and she nodded forward. Christine had been watching us the entire time.

"Who is that?" I asked.

"You mean you don't know her?" she said.

I shook my head no. I pointed to her and asked my friends. Williams got up and said, "It's my date! Christine. She must not know I'm over here. I'll go get here." When he brought her over, her friend followed. William introduced her. He said, "This is Christine Delphinium and this is her sister Wendy."

"The Delphiniums?" Ace said. "Aren't your parents part of the city council?"

Christine said, "Mayor, chief of police and city manager. All of those roles and more are taken by someone in my family." She had the most arrogant smirk on her face as she looked at Samantha.

Wendy said, "Our mother is the mayor and our father is the chief of police. City manager and court judge is taken by one of our relatives."

It sounded impossible. Her family controlled the city basically? No way. But the reactions of my friends said otherwise. The Delphiniums was one of the richest families in the city. Everyone knew Adam Delphinium the city police cheif. But I had no idea they had children. Christine and Wendy joined us for dinner as my friends started asking tons of questions.

For the most part it went pretty well. But Christine kept watching me and Samantha. Samantha didn't seem to notice. She was too busy cuddling against me and sharing dessert with me. At least she was keeping calm.

She took the last piece of cherry cake and held it to my mouth. She said, "Last bite is for you. Or shall we each take a single bite?"

I said, "I like that second idea."

It was cliché. But I had never did it before. She held part of the cake in her teeth and slowly pulled me in. I bit the other part and we slowly met in the middle for the kiss. It was really electric. It was a mix of sugary sensations, along with her signature icy touch. I couldn't keep my hands off of her. Normally I was against pda but Samantha had a way of making me forget about the world around me.

Martinez let out an overly obnoxious cough. Samantha rolled her eyes and slowly pulled away to give him a glare. Nervously he looked to Christine.

He said, "So your dad is the chief of police and your uncle is a judge? That means you can throw anyone you'd like in jail huh?" He nodded towards Samantha. That's when Samantha finally noticed Christine watching me. She wasn't shy about it either. When Samantha caught on, Christine winked.

"They have to have a warrant for arrest," Wendy

said. "This isn't a dictatorship. We can't just haul in anyone."

Samantha slowly made her way back to cuddling me. She started nestling her face against mine. Getting some of my warmth and taking in my scent.

She said, "Sweetheart I grow bored. Dance with me some more. It's almost time to leave."

"You got it," I said.

"Wait," Christine said. "Samantha do you mind if I dance with him? Just one song."

Samantha laughed but didn't even give her a glance. She took my hand and led me away from the table. We made our way back to the dance floor and started dancing. It was a slow song. We held eachother close as we slowly swayed back and forth along the dance floor.

She said, "I told you nothing would happen. Tonight has been amazing huh?"

"More than amazing," I said.

"She's persistent," Samantha said. "Look who's behind you."

I looked back and saw Christine and Williams. But Christine's eyes were glued on me. She still had her flirtatious smile and again she winked. Samantha laughed softly as I spun her around.

She said, "You're quite the magnet. I can't keep these girls away from you. Speaking of girls how is Caroline? I don't see her here."

"Caroline isn't really a big partier. She only goes to Veronica's parties. They must not be here," I said.

While we talked Christine and Williams got closer and closer. She led him. Samantha ignored her but I could tell she knew. As the last song came to a close we finished our dance. It was close to midnight. I took her hand and tried to lead her from the dance floor. She didn't move.

"Samantha what's the matter?"

She pouted. "I don't want to go home. I want to stay with you."

I laughed and said, "Don't worry. It's a Friday. We'll just get together tomorrow. How about a movie?"

She grinned her devious grin and swiftly got behind me. Her arms were around my stomach as she spoke in my ear. She said, "Or we could watch one tonight. In your room. Until we fell asleep."

My heart skipped a beat and I forgot to breathe. I started coughing as I choked on my own spit. She laughed and got in front of me.

She said, "Easy. Take a moment to breathe. Yes you heard me right. I want to sleep the night with you."

"Samantha I…"

"I bet you would have never guessed my parents were both mayor and police chief huh, Samantha? I have a lot of secrets."

It was Christine. We looked back as she stood in front of us. She took a step closer as she stared into my eyes.

She said, "I really wanted to dance with you. One song wouldn't have hurt." She looked at Samantha. She said, "Pretty territorial huh?"

"Very," Samantha said. "That's an odd necklace you have there. What makes it glow like that?"

Christine looked at the cross. There was a stone embedded in the center. When I first saw it, it was a clear crystal. But now it was glowing red. She kept staring at Samantha.

Samantha said, "What are you doing? Why are you looking at me that way. You should stop. I don't like it."

Christine ignored her and kept watching us. Her cross was still glowing red. Samantha shrugged and led me away. We patiently waited for the elevator.

She said, "Keep it together Samantha. So are you letting me stay the night or are you making me go home all alone?"

The elevator opened and we stepped inside. When we turned to the room Christine was a few feet away from the door. She was staring and holding the cross towards us. The red glow was faint as if slowly dying out. Christine was looking at Samantha as if she had seen a ghost. Out of nowhere I had this terrible feeling.

"Hey," Christine muttered. She started making her way towards the closing door. Quickly I started pressing the button for floor one. "Hey!" Christine shouted. At the last minute the door shut. Slowly I backed away.

"You have to be kidding me," I muttered.

Samantha said, "No kidding. That girl is clueless."

Clueless? Did that mean Samantha hadn't seen what I did? Did she not see how Christine's cross glowed brighter when she was close and fainter when she was far away? Or maybe I was reading too much into it. Paranoid. But I had seen a few movies about monsters and demons. There were also hunters and demon slayers. I looked at Samantha as the elevator slowly went down.

"Did you notice anything off about her?"

She said, "Yes. She was staring at you all night. Can you believe she tried to cut in like that? Rude."

"No. I mean did you sense anything from her? Like her energy."

"Below average for a human. That's why I laughed so much. She wouldn't last a second. She's a fly compared to me."

"Oh. Ok good," I said.

If Samantha wasn't worried then I didn't need to be. The elevator finally opened and we left the building. Downtown was dark and quiet with a few homeless people here and there lying on the sidewalks. We parked less than a block away.

I took Samantha's hand as we walked down the sidewalk. I couldn't stop thinking about Christine's glowing cross. What could it have been and why did she try to stop the elevator?

We walked for about five minutes. Then I heard footsteps behind us. Fast steps.

"Hey!"

I couldn't believe my ears. I looked back and there she was. Christine was racing at us and she was fast. Too fast. One moment she was a block away and the next she was close to us. Samantha slowly turned around.

"Get down. She's dangerous," Christine shouted. She knocked me out of the way as she jumped at Samantha. She lifted her dress and revealed black leggings and several holsters on her right leg. She dug into one and pulled out a small silver dagger. She went right for Samantha's chest. Samantha grabbed her hand in an instant. The knife stopped inches from Samantha's eyes.

Christine quickly lifted her leg and kicked at Samantha's head. Samantha held up her free arm and blocked.

"You're fast, demon." Christine said.

"Who are you," Samantha said. "Are you

human?"

Christine kicked with her other leg. Samantha let go and jumped backwards. She landed on her feet as Christine flipped backwards. She got beside me and took two sawn off shotguns from the holsters beneath her dress. She aimed at Samantha.

"Christine Delphinium. Spirit child. Demon hunter and your worst nightmare!"

She fired one shot. As Samantha turned to smoke Christine aimed one gun behind her. When Samantha appeared the gun went off. Samantha screamed like a wild animal. Her body flung backwards and hit the ground.

"Samantha!" I shouted.

It was terrifying and hard to look at. A large and bloody hole had been blown through her. I feared the worst when I saw the wound was steaming but not healing like it did when she fought Isabella.

I said, "Are you ok? Samantha talk to me!"

She said, "It hurts! She actually hurt me. This girl isn't normal." She dug the shells from her chest and tossed them. Her hand was scolding and steaming. She said, "What's going on? I should have healed by now."

Christine said, "No blood no powers. I just shot you with a blood minus, vampire. It takes any pure blood from your body and renders you defenseless. Pretty soon you'll be nothing but a corpse waiting to be sent back to Hell."

Christine was walking towards us with the guns aimed at Samantha. Samantha's left hand looked like a normal human hand while, her right hand had claws. Her left eye was brown and the right was red. She touched her face saying, "What's happening to me? I feel so…weak." She slowly got up but was staggering.

"End of the line!" Christine loaded the guns. Before she could fire I got in front of Samantha.

"No! Christine don't shoot her!"

"Move out the way you idiot. Can't you see there's a demon behind you! She wants you for your blood and nothing more!"

"That's not true! I would never hurt him," Samantha shouted. "I don't know who you are but you're making a mistake. I'm not a demon! I was born in this realm to two humans."

"Liar." Christine jumped into the air and flipped over us. She was too fast for me to react. I heard her feet hit the ground. Suddenly my sight was black and I felt weightless. The feeling lasted for maybe a minute. I was on my feet but all I could see was blurred lights. I felt my body hit the ground as I felt my mind slipping away.

Witch/Warlock

The forest child and spirit child have never gotten along. They're bitter rivals.

Witches, and warlocks are an interesting category of mortals. They aren't monsters, or demons but they walk the thin line of human and supernatural. They are typically human. The exceptions are those who sacrifice their humanity for unworldly powers.

Though they're rumored to sign contracts with demons for power, this is not entirely true. One can become a master of dark magic without devoting themselves to a demon. They just won't be as powerful as one who has sided with the demons. Therefore a witch can potentially side with those against demons.

A witch or warlock is simply a human being who has ventured into the realm of dark magic. They tend to be knowledgeable of magic and curses. Some may be good. Others may be evil.

One who practices dark magic to harm innocent humans in any way becomes the enemy of divine order.

8. Secrecy

I woke up to a bright light shining on my face. I started to scream but my eyes opened first. It was only sunlight from outside. It was shining through a window beside me. The feeling felt all but too familiar. The scent of sweet cherries was all around the room.

I was in Samantha's bed. But she wasn't beside me. The last time I had saw her there was a giant hole in her chest. I called for her and ran out of the room as fast as I could. I ran down the hallway. Then I heard voices and stopped at the stairs.

"What was that? Is someone here, Samantha?"

"Huh? No! No. There's no one here. Come outside for a moment, James. I must show you something."

James? Who the hell was James? My emotions took control of my thoughts and actions. Was it another guy? A vampire guy? I had always wondered why she never let me come over. Suddenly I was imagining her stringing me along while she had some handsome and overly amazing vampire boyfriend. Or werewolf even. I stormed down the stairs.

I saw them hugging and stopped. It was a tall and lean guy with short red hair. He looked like he could have been a courier from the 20th century or something. He was definitely close to her age. Twenty one or two hundred and twenty one. I couldn't tell if it was a vampire yet. I just couldn't get my mind off of him holding her so close.

He said, "Everything will be fine, Samantha."

"Thanks, James. You're the best. I love you."

"That does it!" I shouted. Samantha jumped but he didn't react. She looked back in a panic.

"Oh. You're awake!"

"Why do you sound so surprised?" I shouted.

James pushed her away saying, "I told you I smelled something. It's a human. Get back, Samantha!" He put her behind him in a protective manner. As if *I* were life threatening.

It made my blood boil! My mind left me. I ran at him full speed and threw a punch. All I remember seeing was his hand raising. Then my body was flying backwards. I heard glass shatter as I crashed through a window and onto the front lawn. I felt so winded and weak. It was as if I had fell down 100 steps of stone. I heard Samantha yell for him and I could tell he was coming for me. A shadow fell over me. It wasn't a cloud. I looked to him and I saw his dark grin.

"You smell rather ravishing," he said with a rotten smirk. He looked like he hadn't eaten in years. There wasn't any redness in his eyes. He was due for a feeding. As he reached for me, Samantha came out of the house calling for him.

"Hey! James wait! I want to tell you about Thomas Rouges! He's not a werewolf. I lied!"

He turned to her. "Tell me about your boyfriend after I kill the thief." He raised his hand but I didn't give him the chance. Do or die.

I punched him as hard as I could in the groin. It only pissed him off. After yelling he grabbed and flung me literally stories high. The force behind his throw was so strong I couldn't move my body against the wind. I could only stare as the ground got further and further away.

I started slowing down and the air went back into my lungs. Then I started to fall down like a pebble. Up until that point, I hadn't been afraid since I started dating Samantha. I saw the ground coming to me with nothing to stop my fall. I was going to die. I was so frightened that I couldn't react or scream. I came close but Samantha swiftly caught me. She jumped for me when I came yards from the ground.

She held me in her arms saying, "Are you out of

your wit?" She was smiling.

Quickly I pushed her away. I got on my feet saying, "Who is he?"

"You can't be serious." She laughed.

"It's not funny! Your vampire lover nearly killed me! I can't believe I trusted you. How could you..."

She burst out laughing as she held her cheeks.

She said, "Stop it. Just stop it. You're too much, my love. You flatter me too much."

I grabbed her arm and said, "I'm not joking around! Stop..."

She kissed me. I quickly pulled away but she grabbed my arm. Her grip was way too strong to break and I doubt she was trying.

She said, "You'd fight a monster for me? Knowing you're only human and you'd still fight a monster for me? You really do like me huh?"

"Is this some sick test or something? We're done!" I tried pulling away but she tightened her grip and laughed more.

"Calm your nerve strong man! You have no idea what's going on."

James raced to us. He said, "Samantha why did you save it?"

"IT has a name. Thomas Rouges," I barked.

James stumbled backwards as he said, "What," over a dozen times. He fell over and looked at me like I was some beast.

He pointed at me saying, "Him? HIM? Are you out of your mind? You're with a human?"

I finally pulled away. "Not anymore! You can have her. I thought you were the greatest girl I had ever met Samantha."

I turned away but she was right there. I turned the other way and there she was. I kept trying to get away but she was too fast.

I stomped the ground and said, "Stop doing that and stop smiling at me! This isn't funny. You broke my heart like it was some cheap instrument!"

She grabbed my hands and said, "Would you shut up?" She pulled me in and kissed me again. She held me close and hugged me. She said, "Incest isn't my thing, Thomas."

"Incest?"

She turned me around and said, "Look at his face then mine. Look at his hair then mine. Look at his eyes then mine. Notice anything?"

They both had red hair with the same texture. He had the same eyes and nose. They even had similar grins after I thought about it.

"Siblings," I muttered. "You're siblings."

She kissed my cheek saying, "The greatest girl you ever met huh? No one's ever said that to me and I've lived for close to twenty-three decades. Thomas meet my brother, James Black."

Awkwardly I waved at him, trying to push

through the embarrassment. I had just tried to brawl with him. So much for a good first impression. James looked really mad.

He shouted, "You're out of your mind, Samantha! You said he was a mutt. Not human!"

"I never said mutt! I said moonchild. The only reason I lied was because I knew you would act this way."

James got on his feet and came to me. He glared deeply into my eyes. Samantha shook her head and gently pushed him back.

"That won't work on him. I've tried dozens of times. He's immune for some reason," she said. "And I bet I'm the only one who can hear his thoughts.

He held his head. "That means he knows we're vampires. Samantha this is nothing but trouble. You've gotten this family into so much trouble over this past century. But this is insane! Why can't you stay out of trouble?" He shouted.

Samantha was barely staying calm. She slowly said, "I know the troubles. I trust him. He isn't like the other humans. You just saw him try to fight you for me. He doesn't fear our kind. He won't betray us."

"Betray *Us*? You consider him as one of us? This boy is NOT one of us. He breathes air and his heart pumps blood! This is taboo, Samantha. The one and only rule we weren't to break and you go and break it!"

"She tried to push me away!" I quickly said. "Samantha didn't do anything. I chased her. I didn't know the secret was this big. But I…" I looked at her, "I couldn't stay away. She's right. I wouldn't tell a soul. I'd protect her with my life."

As we stared into each other's eyes, James broke it up. He got between us and looked into my eyes. He was trying to penetrate my mind and hear my thoughts. The more he tried the more frustrated and disgusted he got. Finally he scoffed and backed away.

He said, "And what will Father think, Samantha? What about the three families or the Executioners? Oh. How about lovely Diana? Or have you forgotten the reason we came here in the first place? And now you tell me you fought and lost to a demon hunter! And the icing on the cake?" He pointed to me.

I knew about the demon hunter but everything else was new. Samantha was very good at being secretive. A little too good. I had no idea she came to America because she was running from something.

I said, "Wait. Why did you all come here? You're running from someone. Who?"

"This doesn't concern the likes of you. Your

brain must be frailer than the others if you didn't have enough sense to run from her."

"James enough! If you're going to blame someone, blame me," Samantha said.

He smirked. "I do blame you. Just like I blame you for giving us this curse and dragging us to Hell right with you." He looked at me. "Has little sister told you the trouble she's dragged *you* into? Has she told you the dangers you can never escape?"

"Dangers?"

He got closer. His grin was dark and cold. He had a chilling voice. He said, "Inevitably you will be killed. You should say goodbye to your loved ones. When Father arrives, he will tear your head from your body. Samantha won't be able to do anything about it."

He slowly stepped away as he laughed low and cruelly. I felt a large bulge rapidly shape in my throat when he turned away. The bulge shrank down when Samantha took my hand.

"Don't listen to him," she said. "I'm the strongest out of the three of us. No one is going to hurt you."

I nodded. "Ok. But what was he talking about? All of those people and three families?"

She said, "Come inside. No more secrets."

Spirit Child

Where there is dark, there is light. The monster's counterpart is the spirit child.

Though very divine, spirit children are not pure blooded angels. The classification of a spirit child is this; any human who bears angel blood. A spirit child is born to a human and an angel.

Like monsters, spirit children too have the appearance of a human being but have strength, speed and senses that rise far beyond human capabilities, as well as high speed healing. Spirit children naturally cannot transform. Most of a spirit child's abilities stem from its knowledge of spiritual energy and how to use it.

Aside from heavenly weapons he or she crafts, a spirit child can learn how to summon his or her own unique spirit weapon. If they manage this, they can train even further and learn how to fuse with their weapons granting them a transformation known as angelic mode.

9. Family

"You passed out because I ran us away so fast. It could have been a lot worse, you know."

Samantha and I were sitting at the long and brown table in her dining room. She explained to me how we escaped. Apparently, right before Christine shot at us, Samantha held my head and back and ran us away as fast as she could. Christine was a being known as a spirit child. A mortal with angel blood inside of her. There were several classes of spirit children but Christine was what Samantha called, "Hunter."

"When I first got the curse in the 18th century there was a priest who tried to lift my curse. We made many travels and encountered demons and monsters. He had supernatural gifts. He could use his spiritual energy to fight demons off and even cast them back to Hell.

"He told me he was a spirit child. Spirit children are like monsters. Monsters are mortals who have demon blood in them or like me have been cursed by a demon. Spirit children have angel blood in them or have been blessed by a heavenly spirit.

"Christine is such a being. What's worse? She's a demon hunter. Her powers aren't fully developed but if she were to jump me with her family I'd have trouble fighting them off. Things just keep turning for the worst for me. I can't even sense her energy so she can sneak up on me."

She put her head down and let out a deep breath. She apologized for getting me involved.

I said, "Samantha don't say sorry for something like this. It's my choice to be with you and you shouldn't have to do this alone. We'll get through this."

She scoffed. "Well if Christine somehow beats me she could send me to Hell. Even if I'm not a spirit I can still be sent there with this body. Any mortal can cross planes if they have the right means." She looked so hopeless.

I patted her on the back. "Hey we have to look on the bright side of this."

"What bright side?"

I pointed upward. "I flew today! I always wanted to skydive. And after today I never want to again."

"Shut-up," she laughed. She gently took my right hand. It was bruised from punching her brother. She rubbed it softly asking if it hurt. It looked a lot worse than it felt. Punching a vampire was like punching some hard stone. I felt my bones crush on themselves when I hit him. She rubbed around on my hand. The sharp pain made me flinch and pull it away.

"Not so rough, super-girl!"

"Your bones are fractured! Give me your hand." She grabbed it and pulled me close. "Let me fix you up." She put my hand to her mouth and opened it. Her fangs slowly came out as she watched me with her red eyes. "Do you trust me?"

I shook my head 'yes'. Steadily she bit down and closed her eyes. It felt like cold needles piercing into my skin. Slowly the cold sensation spread all throughout my hand. My bones started grinding on eachother and moving around.

There was a slight pain then suddenly it was gone. She opened her mouth and sat up. I opened and closed my hand. It was like it had never been broken.

"How did you do that?" I asked.

She said, "I gave you a small amount of my venom. Doing that gives you some of my powers. Fast healing is one of them."

"So I'm a vampire?"

She shook her head. "No. I didn't give you enough venom to turn you. All you got is my healing. I would never turn you. I promise."

I looked away. Never turn me into a vampire? But what if I wanted to become one for her? I thought about asking her. But how would she feel about me asking when she didn't want the curse?

When I looked back she was watching me. Did she hear my question? She squeezed my hands softly and looked me deep into the eyes. She looked somewhat bothered.

"Samantha I…"

As I started to ask, her ears twitched. She sniffed the air and looked back in a panic. The knob on the door started rattling. She gasped and quickly grabbed me away from the table. She practically dragged me into the living room and hid us behind the couch.

"Samantha you're going to tear my arm off!"

She shushed me. "My father is here! I have to warn him about you before he sees you. Or he might kill you."

"KILL me?"

She shushed me. "Wait here." She turned to smoke as the front door opened. I peeped over the couch to see her greeting her dad with a big hug. I was expecting a super pale Dracula sort of guy. But he looked really normal.

Similar to James he had on a dress shirt with grey slacks. The one difference was the trouser straps he had on. Unlike his children he had black and slick hair. His eyes were like Samantha's, relaxed and calmed. When Samantha hugged him, he hugged her back with a big smile.

"Ah. Samantha, my dear. How are you?"

"Lovely, Father. Before you step inside there's something I must share with you. It's about my boyfriend."

He stepped inside saying, "The mutt?"

He quickly started sniffing the air. He hadn't

been inside for more than a second and already he had my scent. I ducked down as he began walking my way. Samantha laughed nervously and got in front of him.

She said, "About that. He's not a mutt. Stop using that word. It's cruel."

He said, "I know, dear. The proper term is lycanthrope. You're right. Do you smell that?"

She shook her head fast and got more nervous. "No! I don't smell a thing. How was work?"

He gently pushed her aside. "A human is definitely here. Were the doors locked when you got home? Where is your brother?"

She got in front of him and put her hands on his shoulders. She said, "James is in the basement. I have to tell you something important. Thomas isn't a werewolf. He's something *else*."

He pushed her away and walked towards me. He was getting closer and closer to the couch. I was afraid to move. Samantha's hearing was very sensitive. These vampires were like living trackers. One move and he would have known I was there for sure. I imagined him ripping me in two on sight or throwing me through a wall.

He said, "Oh. Well what then? An imp, troll, incubus. What is he?"

"None of those," she said. "He's a, he's a, well…"

I had to help her out. I was afraid but I did it anyway. I hopped from behind the couch and

173

opened my hands like I was welcoming them.

"A living and breathing human! Hey there, my name is…"

I choked as I spat out the air in my lungs. My eyes were towards the ceiling and my feet had lifted from the ground. His cold hand was around my throat. I choked and coughed as I tried to pry his hand off, but it was impossible. I could feel my bones beginning to crack. He was seconds from literally crushing my throat.

"Father no!" Samantha screamed. She raced to him and knocked him away. I dropped to the ground. It felt like I was going to black out. All I could do was lie there, trying to take in as much air as possible.

She held my face panicking. "Easy! Just breathe in the air. You're alright. I won't let you die I promise. Thomas please stay with me!"

She looked a her father and shouted, "Are you out of your mind? This is him! This is Thomas and you nearly killed him!" If I had never seen her mad before now I had. She looked ready to kill her own father.

He said, "Boyfriend? This is Thomas? Are you blind? He's human!"

"I can see that!"

"I'm fine, Samantha. It's ok."

She shouted, "It is not ok! He nearly popped your head off like a grape! James tried to kill him too. Neither of you are to lay a single finger on him again. Or I will kill you."

James walked in grinning as her father held his head in a panic. He said, "I tried to talk some sense into her."

"Samantha what have you done to this family," her father said. "Do you realize what happens if anyone finds out three vampires are holding a human captive?"

She said, "He's not a prisoner! He's with me. You two are the ones trying to kill him! I've never laid a hand on him."

They started shouting back and forth. James stood there shaking his head in annoyance. There was more talk about the mysterious Diana, Executioners and now there was three families. Then James mentioned Christine and the rest of the Delphiniums.

Her dad shouted, "A demon hunter! You drew attention from a spirit child? How can you be so reckless?"

"It was a school dance! I did nothing out of the ordinary. How was I was supposed to know a demon hunter was there? I'm doing high school things to blend with the humans like you told me to!"

He said, "I said blend! Not date humans and attract demon slayers. We have enough trouble from your ex's lover trying to hunt us down. Now we have to worry about demon slayers knocking on our door! The only way this ends is by him dying." He stepped towards me.

"No!" Samantha said. Her voice had gotten dark and angry. Her eyes were getting redder like they did when she fought Isabella. She pushed me far away. I could see red energy outlining her body as her fangs and claws came out.

She was seconds from going berserk again and she knew it. That's why she pushed me away so she couldn't hurt me if she lost control. She was willing to slaughter her own family for my sake.

She said, "No one is going to kill him! I love him."

Her father looked fearful but he stood his ground. However James slowly backed away. He even knocked over a vase after bumping into a shelf.

"Samantha you need to control your anger," he stuttered.

Samantha said, "For the first time since I've gotten this…curse. I've finally met someone who can see what I thought was forever forgotten. Me. He sees who I was before I got this curse. He's not afraid of what I am or what I'm capable of. He sees what no one has for two hundred years."

She looked to me, "I've fallen for you and I am in love with you. You make me happy to be me. Vampire or not." She looked to her father. "If you kill him. You will have to kill me first."

She looked at me as I gently pulled her back. "No Samantha. You can't hurt your family. Not for me."

Her red aura dimmed as she turned to me.

He said, " What do you mean? Don't you realize they could kill you like you're nothing? Let me protect you!"

I shook my head and got in front of her. "You can't protect me from everything. Even if you are a vampire. I won't let you kill your own family for me. This is something I have to face by myself for you." I looked to her Father. "I love her too. But if you think killing me is the best way to keep her safe then fine."

Samantha gasped. "Don't be a fool! Thomas don't do this!" She sounded as if she was crying.

I watched her father as he walked to me. He grabbed me by the shirt and slowly pulled me in. Samantha pleaded for him to stop as he gazed into my eyes. Just like James, he tried to penetrate my mind and rattle my nerves. But his cloud of fear never made its way to my heart. All I could feel was my desire to stay by Samantha.

He said, "Impossible. I can't read your mind. And you don't seem frightened."

"Only I can hear his thoughts," Samantha said. "Now leave him alone!" She tried getting in between us but I didn't let her. I pushed her aside and watched her father. She said, "You've done enough to prove yourself! Now let me handle this."

I ignored her, as he got closer. He dwarfed me in height, standing nearly six feet tall. Bravely I held my hand out. "It's nice to finally meet you, sir. Samantha is a rare person. I'm glad I met her."

Our eyes were locked on each other. The room was silent and all that could be heard was the slow scratching of Samantha's nails. She was scratching her jeans, nervously trying to anticipate her father's next move. I didn't dare take my eyes from his. When his hand moved up, my body nearly filched. But I stood like a mountain.

"No," Samantha shouted. She took a single step forward with her sharp claws ready. But she stopped when she realized her father was shaking my hand.

"Samuel Black," he said. "You're either very brave or very stupid."

Samantha finally took a breath. She came to me and held me tight. Samuel held his head and started walking back and fourth.

"Father! What are you waiting for?" James said. "Kill him!"

"I can't," Samuel said. He looked at me saying, "And it's not because of this *love* you two say you have for one another. Diana has caught Samantha's scent again. She's on her way. The Executioners called today. They're coming to intercept her."

"Diana?" Samantha said. "But how?"

I had no idea Samantha had an ex. She told me that she hadn't been with anyone for two centuries. Now I had just found out she was being hunted by her past lover's lover. Then there was this Executioners organization I had never heard of.

When she heard the name, Diana, she looked disturbed. Who or what was Diana?

Samuel said, "If we kill him people would wonder where he was. The Executioners would track his death to us."

"You don't need to kill him!" Samantha pleaded. "He won't tell anyone."

I finally got the nerve to ask, "Who are the Executioners?"

James explained. Certain beings had been deemed too dangerous to live amongst humans sometime ago. During this decision a monarchy made of three families was formed: Maria, Rose and Sina. The purpose of the monarchy was to protect humans from dangerous beings and regulate laws for these creatures. Those who failed to obey those laws were punished and possibly executed.

The Rose family was in charge of executing laws. Within the Rose family were the Executioners. They were a group of highly skilled creatures called, Runes. James didn't say much about the appearance or skills of a rune. But he did say they were the most feared group in Nightingale. Now they were going to pay Samantha and her family a visit. Samantha urged her family to trust me.

Samuel said, "It's not him I'm worried about. Samantha we have to think about Diana and this demon hunter you speak of."

I said, "Don't worry about Christine. I can talk to her and explain to her that Samantha isn't a demon.

But what do we do about this new vampire, Diana?"

James let out an obnoxious laugh. He said, "Vampire? You really are clueless aren't you? You mean Samantha hasn't told you about her last boyfriend's lover?"

"James enough," Samantha said.

He smirked and walked closer. "Tell him why she's after us. Tell him what you did to your last lover when you lost control of what's inside of you." He pointed at her chest. "That fiend that you try to hide. If you trust him so much then tell him the truth."

She hesitated to look at me. When I asked about it, she turned away.

"Thomas. We need to leave," she said. "The Executioners may show up at any time."

Samuel agreed. He said, "Smart call. His scent can't be here when they arrive. Take him far away."

She shook her head and said, "Thomas. Let's go." Before I could ask she quickly walked to the door. As we started to leave James called for her.

He said, "You aren't human anymore. You never will be again. You are a monster. A fiend of the night."

I saw her cringe as she looked away. It killed her to hear that. James went on. "Thomas. If you know what's good for you, end things with her. You don't belong in our world. She is a fiend. You..."

"Don't ever call her that again!" I shouted. "Samantha isn't a fiend. She's done a lot of brave

180

things for me. If she's damned then she's the only Heaven I ever want to see. There isn't anything evil about her."

I took her hand and led her outside. It was close to noon on a Saturday and it hit me that I had no idea where we were going. But for Samantha's sake I acted as if I did. She had gotten quiet. Her brother's cold and harsh words had gotten to her.

"You aren't a fiend," I said. "Don' let him or anyone else get to you. You're amazing Samantha Black."

She held me close and rubbed her face against my chest like she was some small mammal.

She said, "Thank you, Thomas. You're so brave. Standing up for me like that. I'm always trying to protect you but the truth is, you're my superhero. I don't know how things would be if you never brought this light into my life. You save me from myself."

Out of the blue she pounced me. She tackled me to the ground and started to playfully attack and wrestle me. Samantha's unique way of showing her affection. Right there in the grass we tossed and turned as we wrestled to get on top of the other. With her superhuman strength, she always ended up winning. She held me down and pecked my cheek repeatedly and growled playfully.

Overtime I found that Samantha was very ticklish in the stomach area. Whenever I grabbed or tickled her there she got weak from laugher. So that was my favored defense against her when we wrestled.

Even though a demon hunter was after her and this mysterious Diana was stalking her, I still managed to make Samantha laugh and smile. I liked how I was able to do that for her. Make her smile when things looked so dark and hopeless. She did the exact same thing for me.

We lied there in the grass staring at the clouds. She was closely nestled into my arms.

"Where will we go," she said. I raised my eyebrow as she looked at me. "We can't stay here. They'll come and find us."

"I thought I would just go home until they came and left," I said. "Hey what were they saying about your ex and Diana? What was James talking about?"

She sat up on her knees saying, "Hmm. Fine. I will tell you under one condition. Let me stay with you at your home until Diana is dealt with."

I knew it made me blush. I looked away, "Stay with me? Samantha I, my dad would flip and…"

She said, "Oh you're eighteen. Don't be so nervy. You can sneak me in. You know I'm like a ghost. They won't know I'm there."

Caroline was the first and only girl I had ever done anything with. But I never snuck her in or anything. Later that night, Samantha would be the first. She had a point about being able to protect me. The truth was I just wanted to be close to her. When the sun went down we went to my home.

All of the lights were off. As I slowly drove to the driveway I turned off the headlights. Suddenly the car jerked and halted. Samantha had stepped out before I stopped the car again. She was racing towards the house excited like a kid going to a playground. But I was freaking out. I shut the car off and raced to her. Before she could step on the lawn a grabbed her.

"What are you doing," I whispered loudly.

She said, "Going inside! I'm tired and I want to rest."

"Samantha I have to make sure everyone's asleep if I'm going to *sneak* you in."

She pointed to the second floor. She said, "You left your window open. Check this out."

I tried to stop her but she completely vanished. No black smoke that time. She blended with the shadows under the moonlight. I heard her whisper my name as she waved from inside my room. She had her ways of making me think, "Damn. She's so cool."

I laughed and quietly went into my home. All of the lights were off and it was dark. After checking my father and sister's room, I went to my room. Samantha was still leaning on the window, watching the sky. Lucky for us, everyone was asleep. It was easier to sneak her in than I thought it would be. Though it shouldn't have been a shock. Samantha was a master of stealth.

I said, "Have you been staring out the window

this whole time," I said. She didn't answer me. It was like she hadn't heard me. She lied back into my arms as I held her and kissed me. Without any warning though, she looked out the window again.

"What's the matter," I asked.

She scoffed. "Your ex is very annoying."

I said, "Ex? You mean Caroline. I haven't talked to her in weeks."

She held her hand out of the window and pointed. I couldn't believe it at first. But Caroline's car had been parked down the street from my home. Had she been stalking us?

Samantha said, "She was here before we arrived."

I said, "I can't believe she's being this weird. Ok. I'll handle it."

"No," she said. "She'll get tired and leave soon. Just lie with me. We need to talk."

She led me to the bed. We both sat there silently. Samantha watched the ground with this really depressed look on her face. It was like we were at some funeral. Grief filled the room like a heavy shadow. Samantha held my hand softly. She finally told me the story of how she became a vampire.

Monster

Most look human until they're in privacy. A monster takes the form of a human, but can turn into something more terrifying.

Not to be confused with a demon, the classification for a monster is this is this; any human who bares demon blood within them. A monster is a child born to a mortal and demon.

 They commonly bare the appearance of a human being but have strength, speed and senses that rise far beyond human capabilities and high speed healing. Some monsters have the ability to transform into an even stronger version of themselves but lose their human appearance upon transforming. Most monsters can learn to control their transformation and go back and forth between human and monster form at will.

10. 200 Years Before

Samantha Black was born February 7th 1796. For eighteen years she enjoyed an ordinary life and grew up on a farm. She loved knitting, horse taming and cattle raising. Her mother died giving birth to her so she took on the cooking and clothing prep when she was old enough. For fun she played twelve instruments but fell in love with the harp. She also loved ballet. In a nutshell she lived a pretty normal life.

Her father didn't let her court too many boys. He made her focus on writing, reading and her instruments for the most part. When she wasn't raising plants or cattle, she was normally found studying somewhere near her father's barn. But when she was old enough he wasn't able to keep her from courting. When Samantha was 17 her father allowed a boy to court her for the first time. His name was Lucas Hellinger.

She fell for him almost instantly. He flattered her in every possible way. Most people loved Lucas because he was so charming. James Black was the only person who felt there was something off about him. But of course Samantha ignored her brother's suspicion. She was too taken by the words and touch of her first love and first mistake.

The closer she got to him the more she began to see his true nature. He was emotionless and cold. When he did show emotion it was like he was flicking an on and off switch. Pretending.

One thing he was bad at hiding was his aggression. With him being her first lover, Samantha was really attached and when he didn't show any emotion it hurt her. When she begged him to show affection he only got upset, distant and dark.

Samantha's infatuation was eventually swallowed by frustration. She desperately wanted him to return the love she felt for him. Every argument erupted with her wanting to know if Lucas cared about her.

One argument got violent though. Out of rage Samantha pushed Lucas while they were standing on a balcony. She hadn't meant to, but she pushed him off. She watched him fall to his death with her own eyes. But the story gets even scarier when she goes to find the body. It was nowhere to be found.

Weeks went by and she hadn't seen him. She couldn't grasp how the body vanished. She wasn't even sure if he ever hit the bottom. Eventually the guilt ate her alive and she went to his home. She was going to confess to his parents.

But what she found both shocked her and broke her heart. Lucas was alive and well. And with him was another woman, Diana Stone-Eye. They had been together for over a century. Of course Samantha didn't know that.

Lucas managed to sway her to take him again. Eventually she found out that he wasn't mortal. Just like me, Samantha had gotten too attached to care. She accepted his darker side. The difference though was that Lucas was far from kind. He was manipulative and cruel. Evil. She had to learn the hard way when she tried to leave him for good. She caught him with Diana a second time and the heartbreak was too much to forgive.

But Lucas had become obsessed. Even though Samantha had sworn secrecy, he threatened to kill her. He didn't want anyone else to have her. She kept her distance and hid amongst the humans knowing priests would persecute him if they discovered he was a demon. But eventually Samantha couldn't run any longer. On the night of her 18th birthday, Lucas attacked her in her sleep.

He snatched her out of bed and threw her down. She tried to fight him off but he wasn't human. His strength was too much. When she couldn't struggle anymore, he gave her the curse.

Samantha described the process as a millennium of agony. He took all of her blood to the tiniest sip and left her cold and numb body on the floor of her bedroom. The next morning she woke in a forest. February 8th 1814 was the day Samantha Black woke up cursed.

Lucas justified it saying it was the only way he could save her from being killed by the three families. (This was a lie. Nightengale sanctioned monsters only. Not demons.) Still she refused his hand. She hated him even more than before for turning her into a vampire and changing her entire life. She avoided him at all cost. It drove Lucas insane. He went through incredibly large lengths to pursue her. Even if it meant destroying everyone she loved. She had finally gotten them to accept her as a vampire. Her life had seemingly returned to normal

But one night she returned home and her family wasn't there to welcome her. It was Lucas. He got desperate and slaughtered her family. It tore her apart. He stood over her dead family as they lied in pools of their own blood.

"Now I am all that you have, my rose." He said.

Samantha lost herself that night. She got lost in rage and slaughtered Lucas. It was the first time she went berserk. She didn't remember the fight. She just remembered waking up with his head in her hands and his blood on her dress. The story was sad to hear and I could tell Samantha had a rough time telling it.

I said. "So then you turned your family into vampires?"

She shook her head. "It was the only way I knew how to bring them back. I had just gotten them to love me again. Losing them like that and being completely alone. I couldn't bear it. I know you must think I'm despicable. I cursed my own family."

We were lying in my bed staring at the ceiling. I held her closer and kissed her cheek. I said, "No. I still feel the same."

She said, "I have a demon chasing me because I slaughtered my ex. That doesn't scare you at all?"

I said, "No. But it is hard not to worry about you now. You've been through so much."

She laughed weakly like she was holding tears back. She said, "It's even worse when you know your days aren't numbered. It's funny. You're the best and worst thing that has happened to me. Time will take you from me someday."

I kissed her. "Think positive. I have a lot of years left in me. Besides if I want I can become a daywalker too right?"

"What? No! Absolutely not," she shouted. She said, "You don't want to live a lonely and miserable life like mine. Don't curse yourself. You don't know what it's like to live alone forever."

I looked at her and said, "Alone? If I became a vampire I'd be with you. We'd make great memories forever."

She took a while to speak. She just lied there looking me in the eyes with her mouth partly open. She said, "You see the best in everything don't you?" Finally she smiled and relaxed in my arms.

As I slept the thoughts lingered in my mind. Becoming a vampire and living with Samantha for an eternity. It felt so dreamlike. Yet I knew it was a possibility. The proof was resting on me. I could live that feeling forever. I starting dreaming what that would be like. But then the weirdest thing happened. In the midst of my dreams Caroline appeared.

There was something different about her. Different yet familiar. It was something I had somehow missed for the entire eighteen years I had known her. In my dream she had confronted Samantha. They had this standoff and just stared each other down.

I screamed for Samantha to stop when she showed Caroline her piercing red eyes. But Caroline never even flinched. She grinned showing fangs similar to Samantha's.

That's when I woke up. I sat up in bed gasping for air, trying to brush the bad dream away from my thoughts. I realized that it was morning. I saw Samantha walking to the door. She left me a note from Caroline that basically said she wanted me back.

Samantha paused at the door and said, "I didn't expect you to wake this early."

"Samantha you're leaving? Why and what's with this letter?" I said.

She said, "Caroline stayed until the sun rose. For you. She loves you. She can also offer you things I never can. She's alive. I'm not."

I said, "But I don't care about that!"

"I do!" She shouted. "I'm dead and I will never breathe air. I can't even cry for you. People will hate and flee me each day I pass them. I can't even DIE. I have to live like this forever!"

I stood up and tore the note into pieces. I walked to her and held her. She was afraid of ultimately losing me. She said, "Why are you going through all of this just to be with a monster?"

Before I could answer, my sister called for me from downstairs. Someone was at the door for me.

Samantha said, "Aren't you going to go see who it is?"

I said, "You're more important. Samantha you can't just leave. I don't care what you are. Can you just stay and we talk about this?"

My sister called again. I couldn't risk her coming up and finding Samantha. So I told Samantha to wait and left my room. I'd see who it was at the door and tell them to come back later. I quickly went downstairs. I was surprised when I opened the door.

I said, "Williams what are you doing here?"

He was just standing there, watching the ground and fidgeting his hands. I asked if he was ok. When he heard my voice he looked up like he had just heard me.

He said, "Just fine. But are you? No one's seen you for most of fall break. Are you mad at us?"

"Of course not. I met Samantha's family the other day. I've just been busy with her."

He looked a little disturbed when I said that. He rubbed his shoulder and looked away. "Oh. Samantha. Is she in there?"

Any other time I would have let him inside. But with the whole red glowing eyes and intense energy Samantha was giving off I couldn't. He would know something was wrong. I kindly nudged him outside and slightly closed the door behind me.

I said, "I'm pretty tired. Could you come back later?"

He looked at his watch and said, "It's pretty early. Sorry. It's just everyone thinks something is wrong with Samantha. Even my girlfriend, Christine."

The second he said her name it was like time froze. Christine Delphinium, spirit child and demon hunter. All I could think about was how she shot Samantha in the chest and nearly killed her. If Christine was a spirit child then all of the Delphiniums must have been. But did Williams know his girlfriend was a demon hunter?

He said, "Everyone thinks she's dangerous. Christine said Samantha attacked her at prom when she asked to dance with you?"

"Williams that's insane. No one fought. Samantha was with me the whole time." I said. "Now I seriously need to go back to sleep."

I tried to close the door but he stopped it with his foot. I didn't expect that from him. He forced himself inside my home uninvited. I couldn't bring myself to kick him out. I stood there patiently, hoping Samantha hadn't went away.

He said, "Thomas talk to us! You keep dropping from the face of the Earth. Even your ex worries. She thinks something is off about Samantha too. I'm telling you she's hiding something!"

"She's not!" I shouted. "She's normal. Just normal! Everyone harasses her but me. That's why she's so closed off. Sorry but I need you to get out of my house. I'm tired. You woke me up."

He kept arguing with me. The more I tried to get him to leave the harder he persisted. I still needed to talk with Samantha. After repeatedly telling him to go home he gave up and started to leave.

But then my sister Marie walked out of the kitchen inviting him for breakfast. The morning

193

kept getting worse by the hour. I couldn't just tell him to leave after that. He was my friend.

I said, "Ok. We'll talk. Let me change into my day clothing."

As I made my way up the stairs my sister said, "Samantha can come down too. There's plenty for everyone."

"So she's here," Williams said. He looked hurt and betrayed. He knew I was blowing him off for her. But it was way deeper than that. How could I tell him the truth? I went upstairs and quickly ran into my room. I shut the door behind me.

"My friend is here," I said frantically. "And he's dating the demon hunter that almost killed you!"

She was lying on the bed, slowly kicking the air and playing with her feet.

"That's nice," she said with a casual smile.

"No," I said. "Not nice. He might tell her that you're here. Sorry but you have to go home. Only until he leaves."

She sat up on and smiled. She said, "You're going to make me leave after begging me to stay?" She slowly walked to me and wrapped her arms around me.

She said, "What if I don't want to leave now? What if I want to play?"

I said, "Samantha this isn't the time."

She pinned me against the door and kissed me. I wrestled her off but held back a lot of my strength. I didn't want to hurt her (even though I probably couldn't). But her strength was impossible. She would only tease me as I held her then quickly overpower me and break my grips.

"Samantha seriously," I pleaded.

She giggled and held me close, "You're so jumpy."

Her grasp was so strong. I barely managed to wiggle out of her holds. I said, "Samantha seriously. You have to hide or something!"

I chased her but her speed was too fast as well. She vanished over and over right before I could grab her. Whenever I tried to tackle her I nearly fell as she turned to smoke.

"Oh darling," she said. She hugged me from behind and said, "Are you all out of breath?"

Finally I grabbed her hands and turned to her but she met me with a kiss saying, "Now I have you."

I laughed. "You're impossible."

As we started kissing my bedroom door creaked open. It was Williams. He said, "Hey your sister says that breakfast is ready."

I gasped and looked at him. He was smiling until he made eye contact with Samantha. The sunlight from my windows was shining directly on her. His smile slowly faded as his eyes tried to pop from their sockets. The red glow of her eyes had caught him in a trance. I watched his body shudder as he tried to back away. Samantha tilted her head ever so slightly and that's when he froze in his tracks.

He stuttered, "What is that thing…"

Quickly I walked to him and closed the door. I grabbed him and said, "Look at me." His eyes were fixed on Samantha though. As if looking away would get him slaughtered in an instant. I firmly said his name. That's when he looked at me.

I said, "Not a soul. You can never tell anyone."

He trembled and whispered. "What's going on? She's glowing and her eyes are red. What is she?"

"Williams focus! You have to leave and you can't tell anyone. Not your girlfriend, not our friends. Not even Caroline."

The doorknob on my door was rattling violently. It was Williams struggling to get a grip on it so he could make his desperate escape. He hadn't heard a word I said. It was useless. So I just opened the door and let him run.

I watched from my window as he burst through the front door. He started racing down the street. I had never seen anyone run so fast. He didn't even scream or look back. He kept running until he couldn't be seen.

I looked at Samantha and said, "That's two out of four of my friends you've spooked. Should I call up Tylor and Ace so you can scare them too?"

Samantha laughed and said, "All I did was look at him! I thought my bangs would have blocked the light."

"I told you to hide. Now he's going to tell everyone."

She sat on the bed, preening her claws. She looked at me deviously and coldly said, "Looks like I have to kill him then."

I nearly fell over as I gasped. I said, "You have to huh?"

She laughed again and said, "I'm joking, love. I won't kill him. Your friend will tell people and they will just think he's crazy. Christine already knows I'm a vampire. But who I really need to worry about is Diana."

"The other vampire girl?"

She said, "She isn't a vampire. Diana is a demonic being known as a gorgon. Gorgons are beautiful creatures with powerful eyes. Anyone who looks into them will turn to stone.

"Whoa," I said. "Can they be turned back?"

She said, "Petrification is one of the dark arts. I'm no witch so I wouldn't be able to help the petrified. Which is why I have to take her out before she finds out I have a lover. She's vicious. She'll do anything to hurt me."

I said, "Have you forgotten about your brave and heroic, not to mention romantic boyfriend, Thomas Rouges? You won't be fighting alone. I'll protect you."

She looked at me and said in a serious tone, "Absolutely not. If you ever encounter Diana, run far away. No mortal could beat her. This is my fight."

"Samantha, I'm not letting you fight a demon by yourself. Even if you are cursed," I said.

She smirked, "You don't know the first thing about those creatures. Yet you're willing to fight one?"

"In a heartbeat," I took her hand.

Curses & Blessings

*A human unfortunate enough to be cursed is given the abilities of a
demon and becomes a monster.*
*A human fortunate enough to be blessed can be granted the abilities
of an angel and become a spirit child.*

Curse Though blood is the most common way to produce a monster, a human can also be granted monster/demonic abilities at the cost of severe misfortune. A curse can either be forcibly or willingly taken from a demon. Witches, warlocks and anyone with knowledge of dark arts can give a curse at the price of losing something dear to them. Anyone involved with giving or taking a curse (demons being the only exception) must make an exchange of equal value. Ex; losing one's humanity, a loved one, a limb or blood. A cursed human cannot produce monsters because they don't have demon blood.

Blessing Under rare circumstances a human can be allowed to be revived upon death and become a spirit child if they are deemed pure and worthy. This won't be an option if a person dies of old age. Before returning to their body, a human spirit must complete a series of tests that will allow them to prove their worth and learn how to use their angelic abilities. If they fail they simply return to their original life with a healthy body but no knowledge of what they experienced in the after life. If they pass they return to life with all knowledge of what they learned and a healthy body. A blessed human cannot produce spirit children because they don't have angel blood.

11. How to Kill a Demon

After Samantha told me about Stone-Eye, I started doing research. I had to find ways to kill the gorgon. She told me if I ever saw Diana that I must avoid her eyes and run away. But I wanted to know how to defeat her. Even though she was this practically immortal being, Samantha was my girlfriend and I wanted to protect her.

We would spend hours in the school library after school. Then we would go to the downtown library when the school closed. Samantha would sit patiently or sometimes lie on the desk while I read books and wrote down notes. Occasionally she would pick up a book or read manga to pass time.

She didn't think any of the books I found were useful. I had chosen all mythology books. Even though my odds of finding anything were close to one percent I took the chance.

As I took notes I read stories about gorgons and saw terrifying pictures. There were men, animals and even children who were turned to stone by these horrifying monsters. Even though I learned about the gruesome creatures I had yet to find out how to defeat one. I was at it for all of fall break and even after.

On a Tuesday during November I stayed at the downtown library close to midnight. I thought I had made a breakthrough when the books I ordered came in. Samantha had went to her home to check in with her family So I was by myself in silence getting any information possible on killing demons and gorgons. But the search got me nowhere.

After I reached my twelfth book about gorgons I had still found nothing useful. Over thousands of words had entered my brain. But I had only managed to write down one paragraph of useful information. When I checked the time it was close to one in the morning.

No wonder the library had grown so quiet and empty. Desperately I looked through book after book again and again. They were useless and the more I tried the more frustrated I got. Why did my girlfriend have to be the one with the psychotic and immortal enemy out to get her?

I returned the stack of books I had originally gotten and went to pick out more. I had nearly read every mythology book they had. When I got to the bookshelf I started scanning for books I hadn't read. Out of nowhere a girl laughed from above.

"You amateur. Everyone knows that the easiest way to kill a gorgon is to use a pixie shot," she said.

I looked up and got startled. I hadn't seen her

since the Halloween party. Christine Delphinium was sitting way up on top of the bookshelf just watching me. How long had she been there? The shelf was so high up that she could have went unseen for hours. She jumped down and landed like a ballet dancer.

She smiled and said, "Hello, Thomas Rouges. It's been too long."

I said, "Not long enough. The last time I saw you, you shot a hole in my girlfriend's chest." I put a book back and moved away. She followed me like Isabella used to.

She said, "You mean the demon girl? Yeah sorry. I was actually aiming for her face. But she's fidgety. You have to admit though. My Angel Cannon is a clean shot right?"

"Angel Cannon?"

She got in front of me and pushed me into an aisle. She took out a gun from a holster beneath her dress. It looked like a mini-shotgun but it was coated with purple and black paint.

She said, "It's the C series. The gun draws on my spiritual energy and creates a bullet when I pull the trigger. The bullet it creates homes in on dark energy and obliterates it from the inside out. Mom got it for me when I turned seventeen. Cool huh?"

I started looking for another book.

I said, "I didn't understand anything you just said. Samantha isn't here and I'm busy."

She said, "Here. I've actually been looking for

you. I'm supposed to give you some stuff."

She grabbed me by the collar and started dragging me deeper into the aisle. I tried nudging her off but she never let go.

She shushed me, "Shut up will ya? No one can see this stuff."

She put me against a bookshelf and pulled a bag off of her shoulders. She took out two black boxes and a red booklet called *Monsters and Demons Volume 135: All you need to know about fighting evil.*

"You're joking right?" I said. "Why are you giving *me* this stuff?"

She said, "I thought you came here to find out how to fight demons?" She laughed quietly while she started opening the smallest box. It was a necklace like the one she had around her neck. She put it around my neck.

She said, "Demon detector. When it's clear you're safe. When it's blinking red it's picking up dark energy. If it's red, vibrating and not blinking, the demon is feet away. That's when you use this."

She opened the other box. It was a magnum. It was red and gold. She started playing around with it and aimed it everywhere.

I freaked. "I'm not taking a gun! Stop aiming it like that."

She cupped my mouth and said, "Shush! The point of hiding is to not be noticed. This is an A series Hell-Fighter. It's one of the most powerful heavenly weapons on the market. I literally had to go to Hell to get the ingredients needed to have it crafted. It's not as powerful as mine but it'll do you justice when you need it served."

She put the gun back in its box and put it in my arms. She handed me the book and said, "Page 105 is where you'll find out everything you need on gorgons. Tell Samantha Black she's a dead girl. My parents have given me the order to take care of her."

I stood with her saying, "You can't! Samantha isn't a demon. She's a cursed human. There isn't a drop of demon blood in her. Just a curse. Like you were blessed with your powers."

She kept walking and laughed. She said, "I have angel blood running through my veins. I can give blessings but make no mistake, I was born what I am. And my detector sensed a demon that night. She's lying. Kill her with that gun when you have the chance."

I said, "Samantha isn't a demon! She was cursed by one 200 years ago."

She looked back and said, "Demons lie and deceive. They're very good with charm. Never trust one. She's lying and eventually I'll find her. Kill her or I will."

We made our way outside. I was surprised to see Caroline sitting on a bench near the entrance. She had still been following me around. But she never confronted me or Samantha. Christine winked at me and walked off and left us alone.

I said, "You can't keep doing this, Caroline. Following me around."

She said, "I don't have a choice. Why are you out at the library so late?"

I tucked my new necklace in my shirt and hid the box and book behind my back. I looked around saying, "Studying."

"Oh. Right." She said. "I should've guessed that. More demon research?" She looked at me when I didn't answer. "What? Surprised? I saw them at school. Why are you looking at that mythological crap? You've never been into that. Not until Samantha showed up."

I laughed weakly. I tried to be convincing and said, "I just have a new interest now. Caroline what are you doing here?"

She took a deep breath and spoke, "Have you ever thought that something couldn't exist? But suddenly one day you find out it does? Even though you know you shouldn't bother with it, you do because you've gotten attached."

"What?" I said in confusion.

She continued, "I just think that some things are meant to be unknown because if we found out about certain things we would endanger ourselves with curiosity."

"Caroline what are you talking about," I said. All of the sudden she was talking about mythology and the unknown meant to be unknown. It was like she knew something.

I said, "Has Williams said anything to you? Because he's a liar."

She took another deep breath, "When I was with you I couldn't believe how great things were getting. I never imagined anyone like you existing. But then I realized I couldn't be with you after I went away with my family last summer. I knew that eventually you would be hurt and I didn't want to risk it. But now..." She started tugging at her jeans and grinding her teeth.

I stopped her. I said, "Caroline you're my best friend. That will never change. But Samantha..."

She sounded angry. She said, "I came here to tell you to stop seeing her. She's dangerous. I know I hurt you but I still care about you. You have to stay away from her."

I laughed and shook my head no. "Caroline, you and everyone at school are so wrong about her. She isn't weird or creepy. She isn't a freak. She's way different. Trust me."

She said, "Which is exactly why you need to leave her alone. She is *different*."

She got up from the bench and came to me. She gave me a hug. It was the first time we hugged since summer. I had forgotten how soft and warm she was. Then her scent went into my nose. The scent of spring peaches. I started getting flashbacks of our past relationship. I had to pull away.

I said, "It's really late. Where's your car?"

She shrugged and said, "I walked."

I decided to walk her home and just get a cab from there. Then I would try to explain to Samantha how and why I got demon slaying weapons. The moon shined bright in the middle of the sky.

The streets and sidewalks were nearly empty. Occasionally I saw a homeless person sitting on a curb but nothing dangerous. As Caroline and I got to an ally it felt as if someone was watching or following us.

She said, "Let's go through here. It's faster."

When I looked behind me there was nothing but street lamps and the wind. I turned to the ally. It was filled with shadows with little light but I could see the end. It was a quicker path.

Samantha was at the house waiting so I hurried through the ally to take a shortcut. I had to get Caroline home so I could get back to Samantha. When we made it halfway something moved behind us.

I turned around as my heart raced. It was only a raccoon digging through garbage. I laughed to myself. But quickly my nerves rattled.

I heard a woman say, "This isn't her either. This girl has black hair."

She was tall with pale skin and long black hair. She was wearing a glimmering black dressed that oddly twinkled under the moonlight. Beside her was a short man with spiky red hair and brown skin. They had appeared in front of us out of nowhere. The tall lady laughed and waved.

She said, "Sorry if we scared you two. We're looking for someone."

Caroline took my hand and pulled me close. She said, "Don't mind us. We were just making out."

She turned my face to hers and started kissing me. Her hold seemed different but oddly familiar. It was protective and strong like Samantha's. But the coldness wasn't there. Just heat. She slowly pulled her lips from mine and gave me a glance.

"Did you miss me?" She said.

I had trouble looking away from her. It had been so long since we were that close. Memories from high school and earlier summers kept floating in my head. My heart and body disconnected. Caroline was confusing me.

I felt numb and I couldn't move or talk. When I struggled to move my mouth she shushed and kissed me. The numb feeling got worse and I was completely frozen. What was going on? It felt unreal and my chest was throbbing.

I heard the mysterious woman say, "This isn't Samantha Black. Let's go."

When she said that I pushed Caroline off and gained my senses.

"What do you want with Samantha," I said. No one answered. She had disappeared.

Caroline let out a heavy breath. "She left, Thomas. Let's go."

I pulled my hand away. I said, "I'm with Samantha! Why did you kiss me like that?

Caroline…"

She interrupted me and started shouting. "Can you imagine what Hell you would be in if I hadn't shown up? Why are you out here alone? I tell you. You've been acting really stupid since summer!"

I shouted back. "What the hell are you talking about?"

She opened her mouth to talk but stopped. She looked pissed but her eyes were on someone behind me. I looked back and saw Samantha. They both had the same look on their faces. It was this look of anger mixed with disgust.

Caroline muttered, "Samantha…"

Samantha muttered, "Caroline…"

I watched as the two girls stared one another down. They both looked ready to rip each other apart. I had no idea what was going on. Samantha stormed my way, pushed me aside and got in Caroline's face. Strangely, Caroline stood her ground.

Samantha said, "I told you to leave him alone. Why are you here?"

Caroline started smiling. She even looked cocky. She smirked and said, "Because *you* weren't."

I don't know why she was trying to mess with Samantha. But it was working. There was no one around but us to witness her red eyes. They started glowing as she said, "I suggest you stop following him around, Caroline."

Until then Caroline had always shown an

obvious fear of Samantha. It was because of her gaze and dark energy. But at that moment Caroline didn't show any fear at all. No sweat, no backing up or even a flinch. She kept smirking.

She said, "Then do a better job at watching over him." When she said that, Samantha gasped and got frustrated. She said, "See ya," and started walking away.

Samantha couldn't stop watching her. Even she didn't know what happened. I walked to her as she said, "Did you see that?"

I said, "There has to be an explanation. Maybe your bangs got in the way."

She said, "No! It's like she knew what I was trying to do and mocked me with that ugly smirk! Something is…" She put her hand up in a stopping motion and started sniffing the air. She quickly grabbed me and looked everywhere saying, "Here? Now?"

I pulled away. "Samantha you almost broke my wrist."

I dug into my shirt. My chest was still throbbing. I realized the cross was vibrating. Just like Christine said. It was vibrating and shining red. Samantha was setting it off. I held it to her trying to figure out how it worked. Samantha was still sniffing the air and looking around.

She said, "She can't be invisible can she?"

"Who?" I asked.

She said, "There's less than one percent of a chance of me being wrong. But I think Diana was here. Looks like she left though."

I gasped. I said, "Is she hot with really long black hair that reaches her butt?"

She turned to me and said, "You've seen her! I heard your thoughts. She was here less than five minutes ago. And you're alive! Didn't she look in your eyes?"

I shook my head no. "I didn't get a good look. It's so dark out here. Plus Caroline started kissing me when she showed up. It's like she tried to distract me or something. Wait." It started making sense. Samantha looked more frustrated. She hated not knowing what was going on. She shook her head and said, "Impossible. No. There's no way Caroline could know."

"But if she's a vampire that explains how she just looked at your eyes," I said.

Samantha said, "She's no vampire!" She gasped as her eyes filled with fear. I had never seen her get so spooked. She looked at the night sky and gazed the full moon. Her face instantly relaxed and she let out a deep breath.

She said, "At least that's one thing I know she's not either."

"You're right," I said. "She's just a human like I am."

Samantha stood and took a deep breath, "Diana will find me soon. Let's go back to your neighborhood. She won't attack us if other humans are present. So did you find anything on gorgons?"

I laughed a bit. I wasn't going to lie to her about what Christine gave me. I showed her the book and said, "Well. Yes."

She took the book and started flipping through it. She said, "This is a demon hunter manual. It's rare. You found this at the library?" She flinched back when she saw the hell-fighter in my hand.

She said, "Is that a heavenly weapon?"

I said, "That demon hunter showed up and gave me this stuff. She wants me to kill you. She thinks you're a demon." She snatched the gun from me. Her hand slowly started steaming and smoldering.

She said, "Demons can't touch heavenly weapons. Look. My hand is burning, but it hasn't been obliterated. Monsters get burned by touching them. But pure blooded demons get severely wounded. An actual bullet will kill them. But me?"

She aimed the gun at her head and pulled the trigger. I screamed and flinched back as part of her face got blown off. She fell to the ground. Steam was pouring from her wound. It was healing fast. Slowly she got up while her face started reforming.

She said, "I still heal instantly. Your friend is a rookie. She clearly doesn't know the difference between monsters and demons. Or curses for that matter." She gave me the gun and book back.

I said, "She's not my friend! I kept this stuff so I could kill Diana and protect you. You told me I

211

couldn't because I was only human. But not anymore. I can fight like a demon hunter now!"

She sighed. "We can't argue here. Diana could come back. My dad has a cabin in a woods a few miles outside the city. Let's go there so Diana doesn't follow my scent to your home."

As we walked something hit me. I said. "Wait! Your scent is already at my house. She could be on her way there right now! My family has no idea you're a vampire. If Diana asks if they know Samantha they will say yes! Then she'll kill them."

We went to my home immediately. The entire neighborhood was dark and empty. Only cars and street lamps welcomed us. A shiver ran down my spine as we approached my house. I feared for the worst

Monsters and Demons Vol.*133*

The Night's Curse

Stay away from this curse. It's one of the worst. The price for
immortality is an eternity of Hell.

A human can be given immortality by a vampire either by force or through an agreement. The process is excruciating but if he or she survives, they will be granted the abilities of a vampire. But the price is heavy.

Every living creature will fear whoever bears this curse. Fellow humans will avoid, fear and possibly assault the cursed child. Those who were once allies will become foes.

The daywalker will walk the Earth alone for eternity while always having a thirst for blood. They will wish for death for centuries but it will never come. Unlike their demon counterpart, the daywalker is immune to sunlight. They can roam freely during the day and night.

Spotting a daywalker.

The tell-tales of a daywalker are: cold and pale skin, emotionless eyes and gazes, avoiding people and keeping to themselves or a certain group. Some may have a cold demeanor but not all.

Along with the tell-tales one can tell if they've encountered a daywalker by looking into their eyes. All daywalkers have faint red irises that look black, gold or brown from afar. If they've had blood recently the redness in their eyes become less faint and their hair glimmers when the sun shines on it.

The surest way to know if one is a daywalker is to simply watch them at night. When the sun is down a daywalker can't hide their true form. Their eyes and hair shine red.

12. Spirit Gun
and the Monster

"Dad! Marie!" I shouted

I was running to the front door. Why weren't the lights on? Samantha was right behind me.

She said, "Thomas let me check the air for her scent first! She could be waiting for us."

"What difference will it make," I said. "If she's in there my family is in danger!"

Ignoring her warnings I tried storming in. But I ran into the door. It was locked. After unlocking it I stepped into the shadowy house. Samantha grabbed me by the collar and pulled me.

I whispered loudly, "Samantha what?"

She said, "You're running in the dark not knowing if a demon is inside! Stop being so reckless. Getting killed won't save anyone."

I took in a deep breath to calm down. She was right. I was letting my emotions get in the way of my thinking. I turned the lights on.

I motioned her to take the lead so she could

check the air. She walked casually as she started sniffing the air in all directions. Just in case, I took out the hell-fighter and followed her. We walked into the kitchen.

Samantha said, "Well, Diana isn't here. No one is."

I said, "No one? Did she kidnap them?"

She walked to the refrigerator and grabbed a piece of paper from it. She glanced at it for a second then held it out to me. She said, "Your family left for the week. Diana hasn't been here yet."

"That's a relief," I said. "Well let's get some rest. School tomorrow."

"We can't stay here," she said. "We have a gorgon and a demon hunter after me. Christine might try to get me while I'm sleeping with you and I don't want to endanger your family. We're going to my father's cabin."

After trying to talk her into staying at my home for an hour I finally started packing a few things. It had been a long night and I was just ready to sleep. For some reason I couldn't stop thinking about Caroline. I hadn't talked to her in forever yet she had been stalking me.

First it was the night Samantha stayed over. Now it was her saving me from Diana. Was it possible Caroline wasn't human? I was the only human immune to Samantha's gaze. Certain monsters, demons and heavenly creatures could negate her gaze's effect. But not any ordinary human.

Caroline looked right at her and smiled. She saved me from Diana. What did all of that mean? Most importantly did Caroline know Samantha was a vampire?

I finished packing a bag. My hell-fighter and demon hunter manual were the last things I had to pack. Samantha was holding the gun in her hand. I watched as steam constantly burned from her palm.

She said, "It's been over a century since I've seen one of these. The technology with this one is way more advanced." She aimed it. "It looks like this one draws on your life-force and creates a bullet with it. How is it possible for humans or monsters to use this thing?"

I said, "Maybe it's a special model. Christine did say she had it made for me. Apparently she went to Hell for the ingredients. What a load of crap right?"

"No," she said. "Heavenly weapons are crafted from demonic material like flesh, bone and blood. They're enchanted by heavenly blessings and become really powerful. Only beings with angel blood are supposed to be able to use them."

She aimed the gun at the window and shot a round. A blue ball of light fired out like a cannon followed by neon blue sparkles and smoke. The whole house shook as the energy burst the entire window out. Nothing but a hole the size of a car tire remained.

Samantha looked surprised as she said, "Oops! I was sure it wouldn't work for me!"

"What did you expect?" I shouted. "Look at my wall!" I ran to the wall and looked at the cracks outlining the hole. I touched a crack almost barely. Immediately the cracks grew bigger and the entire wall and part of the roof fell through. Samantha pulled me out of the way before it could crush me. We sat there on the floor speechless.

I said, "You shot yourself in the head with that thing earlier."

She said, "Yeah. I know. I barely got a scratch but that last round blew a hole in your house. I guess it's luck that's not the round that hit me. It was enough to blow me to pieces." She laughed nervously and gave me the gun.

We both stood. I couldn't stop staring at the large tear in the house. I said, "How am I going to explain this to my dad?"

Samantha smiled at me lightly. Out of the blue her ears and noise twitched. She quickly grabbed and pulled me. "Get down!" She shouted.

I heard a crackling noise. It was like thunder. A crimson bolt of lightning barely missed us. It didn't leave a hole but smoke and static was coming from the floor.

"You missed her, Rouges. Now it's my turn to slay the demon!"

Christine was falling from the sky, towards Samantha and me through the gigantic hole in my room. She had two sawn off shotguns aimed at Samantha. Samantha pushed me away and growled madly. In the blink of an eye she disappeared and appeared inches away from Christine.

She had no time to react. Samantha grabbed her by the leg and tossed her towards the house. I watched in horror as she slammed through a wall and tore my bedroom door off. I heard glass shatter and the house shake as Christine toppled in the other room.

She groaned and rubbed her head. "Damn. She's really fast," Christine said.

"Faster than you can imagine!" Samantha got in front of her. I didn't see where she came from that time. She shot her fist back and swung. Christine panicked and moved out of the way at the last second. Samantha's fist crashed hard into a wall. She pulled it out viciously as Christine ran at her with a dagger. She caught Christine and threw her through the wall.

I nearly had a heart attack. They were destroying the entire house. I ran out of my barely recognizable room and into the hall. Samantha and Christine were brawling in the guest room. Samantha was clearly faster, but Christine didn't look like she was getting hurt much. But she was taking a real beating.

Samantha was tossing her around ruthlessly. She was too fast and strong. She grabbed Christine by the arm and tossed her through another wall.

I watched Christine crash through the bathroom wall and towards downstairs. She grabbed the chandelier to catch herself but it just fell with her. I heard it slam loudly on the dining room floor. I ran at Samantha and grabbed her before could jump through the hole.

I said, "My house! You two are destroying my house!"

"Uh…" She took a moment to observe the destruction and got shocked. She acted like it was her first time seeing it.

She laughed nervously and said, "Oops?"

I stomped the ground and shouted, "Don't say oops. stop her!"

Christine shouted from downstairs, "Try some heavenly magic demon girl!"

We looked out of the hole and saw her. She clapped her hands together and slammed them on the floor. The house shook as a yellow circle formed beneath her. The wooden tiles tore from the ground and launched at us like missiles.

"Out of the way!" Samantha shouted. She pushed me into the bathtub and tore the sink from the wall. She started shielding herself with it against the wooden floor planks as they shot into the room. Water from the missing sink started spraying everywhere as Samantha shouted, "I'm not a demon you dimwit!"

Christine shouted back, "That silver tongue might work with him but not me!"

As soon as she ran out of tiles to throw, Samantha turned to smoke. I didn't see what happened but I heard Christine crash into another wall. I ran out of the bathroom and downstairs. They were having a standoff. Christine had two guns aimed at Samantha, while she had her claws and fangs out.

Samantha growled, "Last warning. Leave. Believe it or not I'm holding back."

Christine shouted, "So am I!"

"Stop!" I shouted. I ran in-between them with my hands out. At the same time they shouted for me to move out of the way.

I said, "You two are destroying my house! It's completely trashed! Dad will kill me!'

They both looked around. They were completely oblivious. They were so focused on fighting that they didn't see how messed up my home was.

At the same time they said, "Oops."

I shouted, "Stop saying oops when you break stuff!"

Samantha said, "She's the one who attacked us! Blame her!"

"I'm a demon hunter and you're a demon! I slay demons!"

"I'm not a demon," Samantha shouted.

I shouted at the top of my lungs as they started arguing. Then I took out the Hell-Fighter and ran to Samantha to put the gun in her hand.

I said, "Demons can't hold heavenly weapons. Page 15 of the manual. But monsters can at the cost of scarring. Look." Samantha held the gun up. Her skin started smoldering and smoking within seconds.

Christine said, "It's made from special material you amateurs! It was made without blessings so Thomas didn't need angel blood to use it. It's made of demon blood so of course the demon can touch and use it!"

She stopped talking in mid-sentence and looked drowsy all of the sudden. She dropped to her knees and fell to the floor as Samantha appeared behind her. I ran to them.

"Samantha! What did you do?"

She said, "Relax. I only knocked her out. Let's give her the slip and get out of here before she wakes up. I don't want to kill her if I don't have to." I looked around saying, "What about my home!"

She shrugged and said, "Sure. Let's fix it up before we leave. Where's your toolbox?"

I wanted to sass her back but she had a point. With Christine unconscious it was best to leave. Maybe she'd be blamed. After I got my bag, Samantha and I left.

Her father's cabin was an hour away. It was on some mountains in Catskin. It didn't look as sketchy as it sounded. It was surrounded by trees and grassland. Nice and quiet.

The inside of the cabin was roomy and pretty old fashioned like her house. It was all wooden but didn't let a single gust of wind inside. It was a single room with one bathroom. I wasn't surprised to see there wasn't a tv. Just a single bed and a study table beside it. I didn't mind though. Mostly because I was worn out from school.

She said, "One thing after another. Sorry."

I held her face and kissed her while she rested in my arms. I rubbed her cold skin and took in the scent of her cherry scented aroma. Finally. A moment of peace with her.

It seemed like there was one incident after another when we were together. First Isabella and the witches, a demon hunter, her brother and now we were hiding from a demon. It felt like it had been forever since I just held her and closed my eyes for a few minutes.

I said, "Are you ok, Samantha?"

She said, "If there's anyone to worry about, it's Christine. Poor girl. She never stood a chance. Sorry about the house."

I said, "I should be more concerned about it. But I couldn't keep my mind off of *you*. It would kill me if she blew you up with one of those heavenly weapons."

She giggled, "You big softie."

She leaned in and brushed my lip with hers. I held her as our mouths opened and closed on each other. Slow and softly. The swirls of warm and cool mixed with a cherry flavor made me go warm all over. She held my body close to hers, trying to take in my heat. Slowly she got me on my back and got on top of me still kissing me slow and softly.

She was perfect in every way. How she was quiet

yet loud. Or how she was so confident yet really self-conscious about being cursed. Even her coldness bringing out my warmth was perfect. Samantha Black was like my other half. Her cold. My warmth. She was my immortality and I was her mortality. We balanced one another out.

I wrapped my arms around her. She lied on top of me with her body against mine. Her soft red hair brushed against my face and gave me the shivers. I couldn't help myself from exploring her body with my hands. She didn't mind at all. She laughed and teased me for being nervous.

She said, "Here. Just relax and breathe." She took my shirt off and gently placed it beside me. She took my hands and guided them underneath her shirt and said, "Your turn, mortal boy." She smiled lightly and nodded.

My body was hot like fire. Samantha was a bombshell. Slowly I took her blouse from over her shoulders. My heart raced. She was beautiful. I think she could feel how nervous I was. She laughed and teased me about it. She pulled the covers over us and started kissing me.

She said, "Is this your first time? You're really nervous. I can hear your thoughts."

I said, "Since Caroline, yes."

She stopped and looked at me. "Oh. Hey we don't have to do this. Are you not ready?"

"No! I mean yes! I want this to happen," I said.

She laughed. "What's wrong then?"

223

I took her and held her closer. At first she was aggressive but the more I held and kissed her, the more relaxed she became. Her curse was at its weakest whenever Samantha and I were that close. She seemed like any other ordinary human. My love for her was like some magical shield from her curse.

It was unlike anything I had ever experienced. I felt this unworldly bond with her. I had so many feelings coursing through me. Each breath I took as we kissed, I lost myself with her more and more.

It felt like I was falling. But the fall wasn't scary or sad. It was like this weightless fall. Whenever I was with Samantha I forgot about everything. Stress, pain, troubles and heck even time. All of it vanished and it was just us.

We lied beside each other in this peaceful silence. I felt closer to her than I ever had. She watched me quietly and I could see the red glow of her eyes glimmering against the moonlight. She took my hand.

"I love you," she whispered. "A lot. And sometimes when we get like this it scares me. I scare me." She held her hand out as claws came from her fingertips. She said, "What I am. The thing inside of me. I don't want it to hurt you. Not ever."

I took her hand and said, "All of you."

"What?" She said.

I said, "I love all of you. Including the thing you say is inside of you. Like it or not. Being a vampire is part of who you are now. I accept all of you,

Samantha Black."

She said, "So you aren't upset about everything that's happened since we met? That witch, Christine and eventually Diana? Thomas I destroyed your home. How can you not hate me? You haven't had one normal moment since the day you sat by me."

I laughed. "Normal is overrated. I enjoy every second I spend with you. You blow me away each time you look at me with those eyes. I could never hate someone this precious to me. So stop thinking that I should."

She said, "You're really sweet. Sorry I just couldn't stand the thought of losing you," she said. "If Diana turned you to stone it would kill me."

I took out the hell-fighter and showed her. I said, "One shot from this and that gorgon is a goner."

She took the gun and said, "You have a heavenly weapon but you're still human. There's no way you could match her speed to even aim at her. All it takes is one glance and you're dead. I'm not risking it."

"Well then turn me into a vampire," I said.

She turned to me fast, as if I said a horrible slur.

I said, "I know what you're thinking. But wouldn't that make everything easier for us? We wouldn't have to be in secrecy from the three families and I could fight against other monsters and demons."

She shouted, "Have you lost your mind? I'm not changing you! Forget it. You expect me to curse the person I love the most?"

I said, "But I don't mind! This way we can be together forever."

"I care," she shouted. That time she actually screamed. She sounded really hurt. She said, "This curse has made my life Hell. I wake up every day hoping that by some miracle the curse has lifted. But I never breathe. My heart never beats. Every living thing fears me and I can't even die! I will never give you that life and it's very insensitive that you ask."

I didn't know what to say. She turned away and sat at the corner of the bed. Coldly she said, "Let's make one thing clear, Thomas." She looked at me out of the corner of her eye and said, "I will **never** turn you into a vampire. Never ask me that again." She turned away but she could feel my stare.

She scoffed , "Why are you giving me that look?"

I said, "Samantha this isn't fair. I can't protect you as a human and you won't let me become immortal to protect you?"

She laughed, "Fair? You're going to talk to me about fairness? Was it fair for a little girl to be forcibly given this curse? Was it fair for her family when Lucas killed them? Was it fair that she had no other choice but to turn them or let them remain dead?"

I looked away and said, "I didn't mean it like that. Samantha I'm sorry I shouldn't have said that."

She said, "I'm trying to protect you. You have no clue what it's like. Never letting you know is as fair as it gets. I never asked for this curse. I'm finished with the vampire talk. If you want this curse be my guest. But you'll have to get the infection from somewhere else. I'm not a donor." She crawled next to me and lied down. "It's been a long day, Thomas. Sleep with me and keep me warm."

As I wrapped my arms around her I asked, "When was the last time you fed?"

She gave me her signature glare saying, "That is *not* funny."

I said, "No. It's just I can hardly see the red in your eyes. So I know you're going to have to get blood soon."

She said, "What are you getting at?"

"What if I said I didn't mind?" I said.

She pushed me and almost made me fall out of the bed. She sat up and said, "I can hear your thoughts! I'm not an idiot. I know exactly what you're trying to do. That's not how it spreads!"

I tried to play dumb. "What? What are you talking…"

She said, "You want me to take your blood so it'll turn you. That's not how it works and your blood makes me lose control. I can't believe you're acting like this!"

I shouted back, "Hey! You read my mind. We both agreed that…"

She said, "It wasn't on purpose! I just heard your

thoughts and so what! Why would you do that?"

I got out of the bed and threw my hands up. I shouted, "I love you! That's why. You keep calling it a curse but the only reason we can be together is because you have it! Why can't you see that my feelings for you go beyond this thing you call a curse? Samantha we wouldn't be together if you weren't a vampire. I want to be with you."

She said, "You are with me! I'm right here and I'm not going anywhere."

"Not enough! Not when this can be forever," I said. "This is my decision and my body. I have just as much of a right to say how long I want to be alive as you do. I have the right to say what risks I'll take to be with you. Stop trying to lock me away and hide me from what you are. I love everything that makes you, you."

She held her chest and blushed as I got close. She said, "Your words. Don't do this. Don't be foolish."

I held her close and kissed her. She took my face with both hands as we fell back onto the bed. We were getting lost in eachother. Yet somehow we were still right there in the moment.

I said, "I'm not afraid and I never will be. Let me show you."

She let out a soft sigh as I kissed her ear. She let out a deep breath and whispered, "I'm not changing you into a vampire."

I held her head as I kissed her cheek and neck.

She kept turning away struggling to say she wouldn't change me. I got on top of her as she wrapped her arms around my body.

I said, "Change me." She bit her lip and let out another deep breath. I asked her again but she kept saying no. No matter how good I made her feel she wasn't going to change her mind. It frustrated me. As I tried to get off of her she held me close and tightly.

She said, "Don't you dare stop. Don't be like this. I can't curse you. I love you."

I said, "Samantha I have to protect you. I need you to let me make my own choices. Not have you make them for me."

She took in a deep breath and closed her eyes. After five seconds she let it out slowly and said, "Ok."

"Ok?" I repeated.

She pecked my lips with hers and said, "I will let you protect me. I'm sorry for not giving you a choice. You're right. You do have the right to make that choice."

I gasped. "You'll turn me? Really?"

"No," she said. She grabbed the hell-fighter and said, "But I will show you how to fight against monsters and demons. I need you to be able to defend yourself against them so you don't need me watching over you. Starting tomorrow you will be learning how to fight monsters and demons."

A demon hunter simply banishes a demon to hell. A demon slayer erases a demon from existence.

13. *Hide*

"Thomas what's your deal? Are you high or something?" Tylor said.

It was his tenth time asking. I just ignored him and kept watching the doors that lead inside the lunchroom. We were all sitting at the table we always sat at. All of my friends were looking at me like I was crazy because I was scooting my chair back and forth repeatedly. Excitement would have been an understatement. Tylor asked if I was ok again.

I shook my head and said, "Sure am."

Martinez shrugged and said, "He's weird. Anyway so Stacy..."

He had been talking about some girl he liked in physics. I wasn't paying much attention. At any second my unworldly girlfriend was going to come from our 4th period classroom and sit with me. I got the jitters every day around lunchtime because I finally got to spend time with her during school. But this was a special day for us.

I watched her casually walk into the café in her white tank top and black jeans. She held her bag with one hand over her shoulder as she always did and stopped in the middle of the room.

Everyone stopped to watch my daily *Samantha call*. I would stand up, wave and call her name. She would look my way, smile and wave back. Then she would get her lunch and come to my table. She never got a chair of her own. She shared seats with me.

I said, "I thought you'd never come. Look I got you a chocolate fudge brownie."

She said, "Awe! I love these."

She *hated* them. But every day we would act like overly affectionate love birds in front of everyone. Especially my friends. That was our way of making everyone think Samantha was as normal as possible. We had to be obnoxiously open about our affection for each other. It eluded everyone to the fact that she wasn't human. Samantha ate the brownie in one gulp and cringed to the side.

"I don't get it," Martinez said. "We sit here every day. Why do you always call her?"

Samantha and I had gotten used to ignoring anything Martinez said to us. Mostly because he always insulted Samantha. We didn't even respond to his question.

Samantha said, "I think I aced my history exam. No I'm pretty sure I did. A perfect way to end the semester before winter break."

I said, "That's awesome, babe. I can't wait to

spend Christmas with you."

"Hey don't forget we have to study after school today," she said with a wink.

Study was a word Samantha would use to infer we were having sex after school. That was another way she made herself seem more human. She would wink and say that so my friends would make assumptions. The truth was that Samantha had been teaching me how to fight demons and monsters all month. That was our *studying*.

I said, "Maybe this time I'll get you. I got pretty close yesterday."

She said, "Well you're definitely lasting longer. Faster too."

Tylor threw his hands up and groaned. "Every day! Come on. I lose my appetite every day. Keep that stuff to yourself."

Samantha said, "History makes you lose your appetite? Because that's what we're talking about. Studying the war."

They were pretty easy to trick. All of them except Williams. He hadn't forgotten what he had seen. Since the day he saw the real her, he never looked at Samantha. But it was obvious he never said anything to the others. They seemed pretty clueless. Martinez still thought Samantha was creepy because of the mind reading incident. But Ace and Tylor were clueless. Being around Williams made me really worry though. No matter how much we pretended, the fact was that he saw what Samantha was.

As usual he got up saying, "Um. Guys I need to go."

Martinez grabbed him and said, "Williams! This is the fifth time this week you've bailed. What's your deal?"

Williams hesitated to talk and looked at me. He didn't have the nerve to glance at Samantha. I could tell he was avoiding her eyes. He turned away and said, "It's Christine. She's my girlfriend now and I just see her a lot. You guys can get that. Especially you, Thomas."

I shook my head yes. Samantha and I watched him while he left. Samantha whispered in my ear, "Do you think she's told him? I never hear his thoughts when he's around us. He clears his mind."

I whispered back. "Do you think she's using him to get to you?"

"It's possible," she said. "I'm not sure. But I can find out. This is our last day before winter break so I'll talk to her."

The bell rang and ended the lunch period. While the dozens of students started leaving I started packing my things. Martinez and Ace left fast after saying bye to me. Samantha stood there watching me.

"What?" I said.

She said, "You plan to talk to the demon hunter? Here?"

I shrugged. "Sure, why not?"

She looked around, checking to see if anyone was watching or listening. She said, "You have this habit of acting on impulse. I'm just afraid it does you more harm than good. Don't do anything reckless."

"Samantha relax," I said. "I'm not a little kid. We should get to our classes before we're late again."

She shook her head and nodded. We held hands and made our way out of the café. Walking in the halls got scary sometimes. Christine had a huge family. There was seven of them. Whenever she and I walked the halls we always saw at least two of them. They were stalking Samantha. I could tell it made her nervous.

As we made our way to the math room we passed Christine for a fifth time. She never said a word when we saw her. She would be leaning against a wall with her arms crossed. All she would do is smirk and wink at us. It was like some sort of subtle threat. All of the Delphiniums did it.

Samantha grid her teeth and clenched her fists. She said in a low voice, "What are they planning? They keep following us but they never say a word. I can't even hear their thoughts."

Finally we were at the math lab. It was time for

us to part until the end of the day. She gave me a hug and a kiss and whispered, "I'm with you. Even when I'm not there. Don't do anything reckless."

I nodded and said, "Don't worry about me. I'll see you later."

I watched her walk inside. Once she was seated I started walking towards the library. I was a student aid during my 5th period. Mostly I just got on the computer being unproductive, unless there was early dismissal passes or letters to handout. Most of the time my walks were fine. But not today. The Delphiniums appeared everywhere I walked.

I would see one standing against a wall. Then another at a drinking fountain. All they did was watch me in silence. Samantha said it was best not to confront any of them and just ignore them.

But that was easier said than done with how much I cared about Samantha. Especially when I saw Christine. They were hunting her. I couldn't just stand there and do nothing.

Christine appeared by the library as I got close to it. One minute the hall was empty. Then this swift wind shot passed me and blew papers everywhere. She was in front of me just smirking.

"Rouges," she said. "It's been way too long. You still haven't killed that fiend?"

I said, "Don't call her that!" I grabbed her and pinned her against the locker. Immediately her siblings showed up out of nowhere. Three on each side of me. Even though I was outnumbered I kept her pinned and tightened my grip.

I said, "You guys have been stalking my girlfriend for the past two months. What's wrong with you?"

She laughed and said, "Stalking? You idiot. We're watching over you."

"Watching over me?"

She put her hand up and held her middle finger back with her thumb. She put it to my chest and flicked her finger. It flung me back hard into a locker and knocked all of the wind out of me. I fell to the ground trying to catch my breath. I tried calling for Samantha but I was choking. So I thought it as hard as I could.

"Samantha! The hunters just ambushed me near the library. Hurry!"

I saw one of the siblings watching me. Somehow he realized I was calling for her with my mind. He shook his head and said, "No way."

He clapped his hands and slammed them on the ground. Blue light started pulsing throughout the entire hall from his hands. It was like some sort of barrier. Half of the hall was nearly filled with bright blue neon light.

Christine said, "Hurry up! I can tell she's on her way!"

Her brother said, "I'm going as fast as I can!"

"DELPHINIUMS!"

I looked to the right side of the hallway. Samantha was storming towards us like lightning. The blue light reached her and I didn't know what it meant until she dropped to the ground screaming. She rolled and tossed on the ground like a wild animal as her skin started shining and burning.

"Samantha!" I shouted.

Quickly she turned to black smoke and vanished. She appeared several feet away from the barrier. But her body started healing immediately.

Christine said, "Nothing evil can get inside, demon. You're welcome to step through again. But you'll be burned alive." She laughed and started walking towards me.

Samantha shouted, "You want me? Here I am! Leave him out of this." She ran to the barrier but The moment she touched it, she was electrocuted and thrown backwards. All she could do was watch.

Christine looked to one of her sisters and said, "Are all the humans asleep. We don't want casualties."

She shook her head, "They should be out for fifteen minutes. Just like you asked."

"Good," Christine said. She looked at me and said, "Stand up. We're going to fight."

"Fight?" I said. I looked to Samantha.

Samantha shouted, "You cowards! Don't make him do this! He's a human. This is against your beliefs! Spirit children are sworn protectors of the mortal realm."

Christine said, "But he doesn't want to be a mortal. Right vampire boy?"

I gasped. There was no way she could have known that unless she stalked us to the mountains. When I looked towards her I saw her foot fly towards my face. My head started ringing as I fell over.

Samantha roared violently and stomped the ground. It felt like the building was going to fall down as it trembled. Samantha was unworldly strong and ferocious when she lost control. I looked her way. She was clawing away at the barrier as she screamed for Christine to stop.

Christine ignored her and told me to stand up. I got on my feet and ran at her. She moved out of the way swiftly and kneed me in the stomach. She moved so gently. Like a ballet dancer.

Yet it knocked the wind out of me for the second time. I gasped for air as my knees shook. It felt like I was going to faint but I still swung at her. She looked surprised but moved out of the way.

I felt the air go back in my lungs and kept attacking. I swung again but she kept dodging me like I was moving in slow motion. She laughed and toyed with me by putting her arms behind her back. She kept them crossed while she repeatedly ducked and dodged me.

She smirked and said, "Impressive. But…" She finally used her hands to block me. Then planted a fist right on my mouth. It was excruciating. I stumbled back and held it with both hands trying to muffle my screaming. I could feel the blood of my lips seeping on my hands.

Christine said, "Too slow. You're not even a challenge. Is that all you've got?"

"Leave him alone! I'll rip your heads off, Delphiniums! I'll tear your bodies in half!"

I looked back and saw Samantha still clawing away at the barrier. She had no effect on the shield whatsoever. It only hurt *her*. Her hands were still burning away but it's like she didn't care. I could tell by the red glow in her eyes. Dark Samantha was getting closer and closer to taking full control again.

I shouted, "Samantha stop! Calm down! I can handle this myself. Your anger is strengthening the curse!"

She ignored me and kept trying to break the barrier. The shame and anger I felt made me forget the pain. How could I defeat a group of half angels? I didn't know what to do. I felt so weak and useless. I heard Christine's slow footsteps. I looked and saw her grinning at me.

She said, "I guess we're done here. I'll knock you out, kill the leech and erase the memories of the humans she encountered. Including yours. Samantha Black is history."

She was in my face. Right at that moment I didn't feel anything. It's like I spaced out. I watched her raise her hand. But then she paused and looked surprised.

She just stood there gawking at me. Something inside of me rang. Without thinking about it I grabbed her shoulders and crashed my skull into her nose.

She let out a painful cry and held her nose. She gained her senses after realizing I was jumping at her. I tackled her to the ground. Her siblings came fast and tried to pull me off. But I wouldn't let go. I shouted, "Leave her alone!"

It seemed like my voice boomed throughout the entire school. The building was trembling. But I realized it was Samantha. We all looked back and saw her roaring at the ceiling like a wild beast. It was like she was crying.

She had one hand over half of her face as if trying to fight. Dark Samantha's strength must had gotten too strong. Her hand dropped as a thundering scream boomed from her mouth. Windows and glass shattered everywhere. Lockers flung open as her violent cry vibrated down the hall. It was as like a storm was raging in the building.

One of Christine's siblings said, "The demon is getting out of control." He took off his cross. He held it out as it started glowing white. It took form of a silver long sword. He started walking towards Samantha as he said, "I'll put it down."

Samantha stopped screaming out of the blue. Her scream had turned into a dark and sadistic laugh. Her body had a red glow that seemed to give off static. I knew what had happen. The curse had taken over her again.

Slowly she moved her head towards Christine's brother. She had a sadistic smile filled with bloodlust on her face. She turned to the barrier and raced right through it like it wasn't there.

She raised one hand as she stopped in front of Christine's brother. He dropped the sword and flew at least twenty feet backwards. His body toppled and rolled once it hit the ground. He crashed into a wall and fell unconscious. Her siblings almost attacked her but Christine held a hand up to stop them.

"No!" She said. "She's burning away. She can't survive in here long."

Dark Samantha started laughing again as she walked slowly. She said, "Fools."

She took in a deep breath and screamed. I heard

it for a split second, and then the pitch got so sharp that it couldn't be heard. I got on my knees and covered my mouth, trying not to vomit. Glass and lights shattered all around us as everything vibrated.

I could hear them fighting and screaming in the darkness. Then there was silence. After a few seconds I heard this low and sinister growling. I whispered Samantha's name. Then the lights flickered rapidly then came back on.

All of the Delphiniums were lying on the ground half dead, except for Christine. I watched in horror, watching Dark Samantha hold Christine by the throat with one hand. There wasn't a single scratch on her. She laughed hauntingly and cruelly as she lifted her from the ground.

Christine was barely alive. Her whole body was covered in blood, scrapes and bruises. I could see her hands barely moving and her eyes open. But she was completely worn out from being beaten by Samantha.

Dark Samantha said, "You thought you'd get away with touching him? You thought I wouldn't get you?" She tightened her grip and Christine started gasping for air as she kicked at the air. Samantha just stood there laughing viciously.

"Samantha don't kill her!" I shouted. I ran and got beside her. I said, ". You can't do this."

"What are you talking about? Of course I can.

She tried to kill you!" She said evilly.

I said, "Samantha if you kill her you really will be a monster. This isn't you. Snap out of it!" She looked at me and laughed. "Come on. Wouldn't you be happier if she was gone? One less problem." She placed her other hand on Christine and slowly started to strangle her. I tried to break her grip and free Christine.

I said, "I know you're in there! You have to fight the curse. Samantha, please. You made a promise!"

That's when Dark Samantha flinched away. I reminded her about the forest and our first kiss. I told her about the time at the park and how she learned how to control herself. Dark Samantha dropped Christine and held half of her face.

She said, "Shut-up! Just be quiet!" She started staggering towards me. But her left foot wouldn't budge. Her left hand went to her face and covered her right hand. I could hear Samantha's humanity speak.

She said, "I won't let you near him. You can't have this body."

I got up and said, "That's it! Samantha you're doing it!"

She flinched again and grunted. Dark Samantha shouted, "No! I just got here. Don't make me go back! Damn...it!" She put her hands to her head like she had a bad headache. She said, "Ah! No." I grabbed her from behind so she couldn't attack me.

I held her and said, "Samantha it's over now. Come back. I need you. I love you."

Dark Samantha let out a loud scream and tried to break free of my hold. But Samantha's humanity had overpowered the curse. It was clear to me then. Samantha Black and Dark Samantha were separate. Samantha Black represented her humanity. Dark Samantha represented her curse. She was at war with the curse and I was the one person who gave her the power to beat it.

I said, "Samantha. I love you."

Dark Samantha let out one last cry. While I held her it died down to a more human scream. It became less monstrous and more womanly . She dropped her head. When she caught her breath she looked at me. I could see the guilt in her eyes. Before she could talk I kissed her and held her tight.

"It's ok. I'm right here," I said.

I rubbed her back and kept her in my arms. As we held each other the period bell rang. Students began flooding the hallways. I looked around and realized the Delphiniums were gone. It was as if nothing had happened.

Samantha said, "Where are they? I thought..."

I said, "They must have ran off while I was helping you gain control."

She let out a deep breath, "Good. That means I

didn't kill any of them. Those idiots. They pushed me too far."

I couldn't figure out how they left so fast without being noticed. Students were walking around like nothing had happened. The same thing happened with my home. When Samantha and I went back the day after, it was completely undamaged. As if nothing had ever happened. Before I could ask any questions Samantha grabbed my arm and started leading me away.

She said, "Winter break just started. We're leaving."

"Leaving? Samantha we have statistics," I said.

She said, "You were just beaten by spirit children and you're worried about statistics?"

She led me outside and finally let me go. She motioned me to get in front of her. Since we were hiding out in the mountains Samantha started running us to school. With a car it took an hour. But with Samantha it took ten minutes.

I backed away and said, "Again? Samantha come on. Let's drive ok?"

She rolled her eyes and took my hand. She said, "The nausea only lasts you five minutes. You've been doing well at keeping up with superhuman speeds. Did you notice how your eyes could keep up with Christine's movements?"

I scoffed and reluctantly turned my back to her.

She put one hand on my head and the other on my lower back. Without any warning (as usual) she rocketed off. I felt the force of her sprint push against my body. It felt like a plane taking off. This intense pressure pressed against my body and after a few seconds I didn't feel anything. I was weightless.

At first my eyes couldn't keep up with the speed. All I would see was blurred light and hear the wind smack harshly against my face. But as I trained with Samantha I learned how to use all of my senses to their fullest potential. When I couldn't see with my eyes, I saw things by hearing or smelling them. I could also feel things around me with my sense of touch to some degree. My sense of taste stayed the same for the most part.

It took me all of November and December to sharpen my senses as much as possible. I practiced by watching Samantha race around the mountains. She claimed to be faster than light when she ran her fastest. When I couldn't see her she told me to listen, smell and even try to feel the winds moving around me.

At first it was hard. But after watching her race around for a while, my eyesight improved. My vision had sharpened greatly. But not quite sharp enough to see things moving faster than light.

The point of raising my senses was to give me the ability to fight and defend against demons and monsters. There was no way to raise my physical abilities to match a supernatural creature's. But with superhuman senses and a heavenly weapon I could defend myself.

After fifteen minutes Samantha had taken us to the cabin. The mountains had gotten filled with snow since the third week of winter. Since I didn't have the tough skin of a vampire I couldn't be trained outdoors. Mostly we just stayed inside the cabin.

It was a standard cabin made for two or three people. All of it was made of wood but it was surprisingly warm and relaxing. There was only one bed and a wooden study table. There wasn't a tv or anything entertaining. So for the most part all I could do was sit around, do class work, study or read. The boring stuff.

Samantha was a pro at finding things to do with the silence. She read books, played her harp, knitted scarves and sometimes she just enjoyed the quiet. But I got bored pretty fast.

I sat on the bed watching her tune her harp's strings. She was sitting at a wooden desk near a window. She was really passionate about her harp. She would play it for hours and I never got tired of listening to her play and sing. She noticed me watching for the fifth time.

She said, "Bored? You haven't done anything

since we arrived here this afternoon."

I said, "There isn't much to do. Samantha how long do we have to stay here?"

"Until the Executioners find and kill Diana. Shouldn't be too much longer."

I said, "It's been a long time since we last saw her. How are you sure she's still here?"

She started playing her harp to check the tuning. She said, "I've known the woman for two hundred years. She won't leave until she finds me. I know she's in the city because of her nasty odor. But she's miles away. So no worries. I'm sorry that you're bored but you'll just have to wait this out."

Especially since she refused to reveal Diana's scent to me. Since I sharpened my senses to their peaks, I could smell people from far away distances like Samantha. Fearing I'd try to find Diana on my own, Samantha didn't tell me how to recognize her scent. I had no choice but to wait.

We spent weeks there. It wasn't entirely awful with Samantha being there. We savored every moment of privacy we had. It was nice. Sharing quiet nights with her and enjoying the peace we had.

She was pretty paranoid about Christine though. Every hour of the night she would check the area for her and other hunters. But they never showed up.

On Christmas Eve, we left the cabin for a few

days. Samantha didn't want me to miss the holidays with my family and friends. We still couldn't figure out how the house was completely fine. It looked new. My father hadn't said anything about it, so we figured the house was fixed before he was able to see it.

For the most part things were looking pretty normal for us again. Winter break went by fast and there wasn't any bother from demon hunters or demons. After winter passed we focused on passing classes so we could graduate. It was weird. Christine had vanished. Since the day Dark Samantha nearly killed her we hadn't seen her or her siblings and there was still no signs of Diana. Samantha didn't even smell her aroma anymore.

May came and I was two weeks from graduating high school. Even though we hadn't seen Diana, Samantha still had us stay in the mountains. The Executioners hadn't found her either so Samantha was extra cautious. Things weren't as boring with the spring weather warming things up. The snow had melted away and all sorts of mammals started roaming the mountains.

May 11th, 2017 was the day I saw someone I hadn't talked to for months. It was early so I was still asleep in the cabin. Samantha usually got up early to watch the sunrise and birds sing. Simple things like that fascinated her. But that morning I woke up to the sound of voices. Arguing.

"You have got to be kidding me! You have him out here in the mountains," someone shouted.

I sat up because the voice sounded pretty familiar. I didn't believe it until I went outside. She had somehow found us. She looked at me the moment I stepped out. She ran to me and grabbed me.

"Thomas! I've been so worried," she said. "Are you ok?"

"Caroline?" I said. "How did you..."

She interrupted. She said, "So you mean to tell me you're hiding from everyone on purpose? No one has been able to talk to you in months! You're never home. Your dad says you're with *her* but nobody knows where she lives. Why the hell are you out in Catkin Mountains?"

Samantha said, "We're just on a camping trip. There's nothing to worry about, Caroline. Go home."

"I wasn't asking you. I was asking *my* friend," Caroline said. She looked to me and said, "Why are you being so freaking weird? Since you met her you've been so different. Why?"

I had trouble answering her. I couldn't find the nerve to lie to her face. But I couldn't tell her the truth either. Caroline looked like she thought I might have been dead. She really didn't understand what was going on and she wanted to know. But I couldn't tell her.

She grabbed my hands and begged. She said, "Tell me! Why are you in these mountains? You don't even like hiking. Why aren't you talking to me or your real friends? Thomas, tell me why she's brought you out to the middle of nowhere!"

"Caroline it's none of your business!" I shouted. "We aren't kids anymore. I don't need you to watch over me. Go home and stop following us."

She gasped and flinched back when I said that. It was like I stabbed her in the stomach. It took her a few seconds before she took a breath. Finally she said, "What did you just say to me?"

I tried to be calmer. I looked away and said, "Go home. This isn't any of your business. Samantha and I are on a camping trip. That's it."

"Liar," she said not a second sooner when I stopped talking. She waited for me to look into her eyes. She said, "You're lying to me. Something is going on here and I'm going to find out."

She turned away and started walking to Samantha demanding to know why we were in the mountains. She got in Samantha's face and started yelling.

Samantha said, "Listen to him and leave. It's for your own good, Caroline. Do not start a fight with me."

Caroline got madder. She said, "Am I supposed to be afraid of you, goth girl? I want to know the truth. He never used to lie. Especially not to me. What's going on? Tell me!" She grabbed Samantha by the shirt.

I shouted for her to stop. She ignored me and kept demanding the truth from Samantha. Samantha was staying calm. But it was obvious her patience was dying.

She said, "Caroline. For your own safety I suggest you remove your hands from my collar. You're right. Something is going on. And if you don't leave you're going to find out what it is."

Caroline said, "Let's get one thing clear, Samantha Black. I am not afraid of you. I'm giving you a warning. I don't know why he's lying. But if I find out you've hurt him you will be sorry. Understand?"

Samantha smirked and grabbed Caroline's hand. But Caroline didn't let go. She tightened her grip and glared at Samantha. It was happening again. Caroline wasn't being influenced by the gaze.

Samantha said, "You have no idea who you're dealing with, Caroline. If I were you I..."

"I know you better than you think, Samantha Black." She smirked. Before she could do anything else I grabbed her and pulled her away.

I shouted, "Are you crazy? You stalk me and then try to pick a fight with my girlfriend?"

She shouted back, "There's something wrong with her! Everyone sees it but you. Tell me why you're in the mountains!"

I shouted again. "If you don't leave now I will never talk to you again!"

In the blink of an eye she threw her fist at the left side of my jaw. I fell down hard as I held my face. I couldn't believe she hit me. She stood over me breathing hard. Her fists were balled and her face had gone red.

"Do you think I'm an idiot or something?" She was sniffling and crying. She pointed to her face and said, "Is this why you chose her over me?"

"Caroline what are you talking about?" I said.

She cried, "Mortal. I'm a mortal being. Is that what this is about? You don't want a human girl. You want the bloodsucking leech?"

I couldn't believe my ears. Samantha looked just as shocked as me. Caroline knew Samantha was a vampire. But for how long? She said, "Why can't you at least tell me the truth anymore? Did she make you forget all of the memories we shared? Is that body snatcher more important than our 18 year old friendship?"

"Don't worry, Caroline. In about two minutes, Samantha Black will be in Hell where she belongs."

My body shook when I heard the voice. Christine Delphinium. She was a few feet behind us. She was holding her demon detector in her hand. She held it out towards us and smirked.

She said, "I'm ready for you this time, demon."

Samantha laughed and said, "You didn't learn your lesson the first two times? Go home and let those powers of yours mature. Come back in about two centuries."

Christine kept smirking. She said, "I'm so glad you picked a place so far away from the humans. Now I don't have to hold back."

Her demon detector started glowing yellow when she shouted, "Purity."

The cross, shined white as Christine held it with both hands. Suddenly this strong pulse that felt like a sonic boom vibrated away from her body. It made me stumble back. Caroline stopped my fall and grabbed my arm. I looked at her realizing she was smirking.

She said, "Kick her ass, Christine!"

I couldn't believe what she said. Obviously she knew about the Delphiniums. Before I could question it I heard something heavy hit the ground. I looked to see Christine holding a gigantic broadsword. It had to be at least 6 feet long. The sword had an onyx colored blade with a golden handle. Christine lifted it with one hand towards the sky like it was a feather.

She said, "I had to train intensely to learn how to summon this. Behold, demon. My spirit weapon. PURITY!"

Samantha looked petrified. She barely managed to say, "Impossible. A heavenly sword? Only pure blooded angels can craft those let alone wield them."

I watched in terror. Christine slammed the sword down on her.

Hell Gate

The only way to send a demon away for good, is by sending it home.

A hell gate is a portal that leads from where it is summoned to Hell. Due to how dangerous they are, it is necessary for a spirit child to be a master of summoning the gates before being granted the title, Demon Hunter. Unsufficient knowledge of Hell Gate summoning can result in the release of dangerous demons or worse, Hell on Earth.

All souls are sent directly to judgment upon being sent to Hell. From there it is decided what their fate will be. If for some reason a mortal is sent to Hell without authorization from divine law, they are immediately sent back to where they were originally from judgment. No exceptions.

With Hell being one of three soul realms, time does not exist within the portal leading to Hell. If one wishes to, they can use this to travel long distances, instantly on Earth. This use of the gate however is dangerous when used excessively and if done too often, can result in divine punishment.

The more demons a hunter sends to Hell, the more badges they gain. With enough badges, a spirit child can move up, granting them more privileges and higher rankings. With enough badges a demon hunter can get a promotion if they wish.

14. Clash on the Mountain

Christine's sword crashed on the ground and shook it violently. A large fissure launched from where the sword hit as a gust of red light launched from the sword towards Samantha. Samantha vanished at the very last second and so did Christine. They both appeared in the sky. Christine raised the sword above her head again.

She said, "Say bye, bye, to your mortal lover, demon!"

Samantha raised her forearms in front of her face. The sword slammed against them and sent her flying to the ground. She crashed into the grass as Christine landed in front of her. She got up and I could see large gashes on her forearms. They weren't closing up. Not even steaming.

Christine said, "Those won't heal. Not unless you get sent to Hell. Oh but don't worry. I'm sending you there in about five seconds."

"Fool," Samantha shouted. "I am not a demon. I am NOT a demon! I have the night's curse. A bloodless gave it to me 200 years ago. You have to believe me!"

Christine laughed as she began dashing at Samantha with the sword over her shoulder. She got ready to take another swing at her. She said, "No more lies, demon girl. It's all over!"

She vanished and appeared right above Samantha's head. She used both hands to swing the sword down. Black smoke appeared as the sword crashed into the earth.

Christine let go of the sword and pulled out two red pistols from the holsters beneath her dress. Samantha appeared to her left ready to attack but Christine was already aiming at her with both guns. Samantha tried to change directions but it was too late. She flew backwards as two shots blew from the guns. Caroline raised her fists to the air and celebrated.

She said, "YEAH! Kick her ass, Christine! Get rid of that fiend!" I tried to run for Samantha but Caroline grabbed me and said, "No! Stay out of it. She's dangerous."

I said, "I love her more than anything and you want her dead? Christine is going to kill her! What kind of friend are you?"

Caroline said, "The kind that would protect you from the likes of her."

I shouted, "Caroline let me go! You have to let me help her."

This red light started shining from where Christine and Samantha were. The ground started rumbling and I heard the sound of chains rattling. Two giant wooden pillars slowly rose from the ground and I could hear terrifying howling and screaming. A red and ominous vortex shined between the pillars.

It flickered and rippled in circles. Everything around it started getting sucked inside. Caroline stopped me from slowly dragging inside. Christine walked towards Samantha with her sword on her shoulder. Samantha just lied there on the ground, trying to gain the strength to get up.

She screamed fearfully, "No! You can't! I'm human!. Inside of me is a soul. You can't send me to Hell! You...."

Christine interrupted her with a stab to the chest. Samantha screamed out a monstrous and painful scream. It was the first time I saw her get desperate and afraid. Out of the portal shot dozens of black chains that wrapped around Samantha's wrists. She frantically fought them off of her legs and tried to crawl away.

She screamed frightfully, "I'm not a demon! I'm not! You can't send me there! Please. I'll leave and never return. I swear!"

Christine said, "I don't negotiate with demons. I'm sending you home."

The chains yanked on Samantha's wrists. She fell over and started getting dragged into the portal slowly. She screamed in terror and tried to stop her drag with her feet. But it was useless. She was helpless. She screamed and pulled away as if she was being tortured. I pushed Caroline away as hard as I could and raced for her. I shouted for her. She was getting closer to the portal.

She looked at me crying tearlessly. "Don't! Stay back or you might get dragged inside with me!"

"I don't care!" I shouted.

I came close. Suddenly all of the air in my lungs went out of my mouth as I coughed. It wasn't Christine. Caroline was in front of me. Her fist was at my stomach. I held it trying to catch my breath.

She said, "I'm not letting that monster get near you."

All I could do was watch as Samantha got dragged into the portal. I screamed for her as loud as I could as the pillars went back into the earth. Just like that. She was gone.

Sent to Hell. Caroline finally let me go. I ran to where the portal was. Nothing was there. The grass was completely intact. It was like the portal had never been there. I ran to Christine and grabbed her.

"Bring her back! Bring her back now!"

She pushed me onto my rear and pulled out a

small and silver stone. She said, "You won't even remember her. Look at this stone."

I turned away and shut my eyes. I said, "I won't let you take my memories of her! I love Samantha Black."

"Samantha Black? So she is here!"

We all looked back. I couldn't believe my eyes. We had the worst luck. Diana Stone-eye had finally shown up. Looking at her made me stiff all over. The fear she made me feel was like being placed in a box with hundreds of snakes. She slowly walked towards us and I remembered not to look into her eyes.

Christine smirked and said, "Looks like I'm getting rid of two demons today. Great. I'll get that badge faster than I thought." She held her hand out. On cue her sword rose from the ground and soared to her hand. She caught it and dashed at Diana.

She said, "I sent the demon where you're going. Straight to Hell." She jumped and got her sword ready.

Diana flipped her hair over her shoulder slowly and looked at Christine. Christine's eyes shined neon blue as she said, "Blessed eyes. Your cursed eyes can't affect me, fiend!"

Diana said, "How boring. I didn't come to play with children." She vanished right as Christine's sword hit the ground. She was right behind her.

Christine quickly spun around and started slashing at Diana. But she was moving too fast. Diana was dodging her like it was nothing.

She said, "*You* sent Samantha to Hell? That displeases me. From what remember, she's much faster."

Christine laughed, "Sorry but this isn't exactly your welcoming party!"

She swung the sword but it stopped right before it could hit Diana's skull. She caught it barehanded. The force behind the strike was so strong it made the landscape behind Diana erupt from the ground.

Christine said, "But how? Demons can't touch angel weapons. Your hand should have blown away."

Diana smiled deviously and said, "Well it's simple. Look at my arm. Does it look familiar?"

Christine gasped. She said, "You...you monster. You took an angel's arm!"

Before she could do anything else, she spat up blood as Diana ran her hand through her stomach. I nearly threw up when I saw it reach out of her back. Christine didn't even scream. She was shaking all over as she struggled to breathe. She was slowly raising her sword to take one last swing at Diana but she was too weak.

Diana said, "I've dealt with pure blooded angels once from chasing that girl. I came prepared. No one takes my prey. Not even children."

She raised Christine from the ground and tossed her away like she was a worn out toy. Then she turned to me and Caroline.

I gasped and said, "She...she punched a hole right through her. Caroline we have to run!"

Caroline shook her head 'no' and motioned forward. I looked to see Christine back on her feet. The hole in her stomach was closing fast as her eyes shined blue. It had to be fast healing. Just like Samantha.

Her siblings suddenly appeared around her. Each of them had their own heavenly weapon. Christine grabbed hers and got in the middle of the group.

She smirked and said, "Alright, demon. Let's see how you do against seven half-angels."

Diana said, "I wasn't looking to slaughter an entourage of immature spirit brats. But seeing how Samantha is gone why not have some fun? How will we do this? One at a time or all at once?"

Christine grinned and said, "This one won't be sent to Hell. We're wiping her from existence!"

All at once they vanished. Then they appeared from every direction around Diana. They had their weapons ready as they dove after her. In the blink of an eye, Diana disappeared.

I could follow her movements even though she was really fast. Right as the Delphiniums attacked she had leaped into the sky. Christine was right beneath her. As she swung the blade Diana blocked with her angel arm repeatedly.

When the other Delphiniums realized Diana was in the air with Christine, they joined the airborne battle. Christine got flung downward by a heavy kick to the face. Somehow she stopped her fall in midair and jumped off of nothing and attacked again. Diana was just standing in the air waiting for them to attack.

Caroline said, "Damn. She's a lot stronger than Christine originally said. They can't even touch her."

I looked at her and said, "Wait. You know, Christine?"

She said, "I'm the reason Christine has known where you two are. When I found out you were dating a vampire I had to do something. The Delphiniums were the only people I knew who could beat her."

I should have asked how she knew so much about the supernatural world. I should have asked how she knew Samantha was a vampire. Why was she immune to the gaze? How did she know about half-angels? Was she or wasn't she human?

But all I felt was rage. My hands were clenching her arms as I grabbed and pulled her close. She was shouting for me to let her go.

I said, "You did this! You're the reason Christine

found us at my house that one night. You're the reason Samantha got sent to Hell!"

Caroline shouted, "You idiot! I did this because I still love you. Samantha is a bloodsucking leech. You're nothing but a blood bank in her eyes. Those filthy creatures aren't capable of feeling love!"

I never wanted to hit a girl so badly. Up until that moment I had never wanted to hit a girl ever. And it was my best friend.

I shouted in tears, "You're the idiot, Caroline! You robbed me and Samantha of something really special. You're supposed to be my friend!"

"I am!" She said. "That's why I had to get her away from..."

I said, "You didn't get her sent to Hell for my safety. You did it for yourself! You're jealous of Samantha. She never laid a hand on me. I loved her and you destroyed everything I had with her. We are not friends!"

I didn't hit her. But I did push her away. Hard. She stumbled back and fell. She looked like she was in shock. Her mouth was hanging open as she stared at me speechlessly.

When I took out the hell-fighter she somewhat flinched away. It wasn't for her though. It was for Diana and the Delphiniums. I turned away and ran towards them.

15. Enter, Green

He pushed me to the ground and ended our friendship. He couldn't have meant it. He was just being an idiot. Right? There's no way he could have actually loved that...thing.

I pushed him away because of what I am. I didn't want to endanger him. I did what was best for the love of my life. I never meant to hurt him. All I ever wanted was to protect, Thomas.

I protected him since we were kids. We had been best friends for 18 years. Then we fell in love. So why is it...why did he push me down and run from me? He ran towards the half-angels and demon fighting in the sky.

He held the heavenly weapon I made. Crafted purely with love. My love for him. I sat on the ground crying as he aimed at the sky. That's when I came to my senses.

"No!" I shouted. "Stay out of it. Thomas you'll get hurt!"

I ran for him as he shot the first round. My heart nearly tore in half as I witnessed the size of the bullet. How the gun worked was very simple. It drew its power from the love of whoever held it and created a bullet. The bullet's size and power increased as the person's love strengthened. His love for Samantha was as big as a miniature sun.

I had to stop and watch it spiral towards the angels and demon fighting. It was neon blue and hummed like a thousand birds singing. Beautiful, yet deadly. As soon as the Delphiniums and Diana saw it, they stopped their attacks and scattered in every direction.

"James look out!" Christine shouted.

But he was too slow. The attack was way too massive. He couldn't get around it and got hit. The explosion caused this massive wind to blow down on us. Thomas bravely stood his ground as he aimed again.

He was aiming for all of them. Passionate vengeance. Taking out every last one of his lover's enemies. Was I next?

James fell from the explosion covered in burns and blood. His body was smoking but I could tell he was alive. Heavenly weapons can't pierce heavenly souls. But it can damage their bodies brutally. I watched his body hit the ground as Diana started attacking the distracted Delphiniums.

She took three out in a flash. One fatal hit to each and they dropped from the sky. My heart started racing as she dispatched two more as they attacked her. She used her angel arm to block both of their attacks. Then she vanished and got behind them. Her hair spread out and grew into giant pythons. When they realized the gorgon was behind them the serpents had wrapped around them.

Christine was so worried about James that she hadn't noticed her sisters getting the lives squeezed from them. I didn't know what to do. Even though I could have fought Diana it would have meant Thomas finding out what I was. The thought of him fearing me made me want to die. I was more than willing to risk the lives of angels than letting him know my dark truth. But if they were all dead there would be no one else but me to protect him.

"CHRISTINE!" I shouted loudly. "What are you doing? She's right behind you!"

Too late. Right when Christine turned around one of the snakes from Diana's hair bit her in the shoulder. Christine let out a gruesome scream. The snake brought Christine to Diana by its mouth as the other snakes shrank back to normal hair. Diana took her by the throat and laughed. The last Delphinium capable of fighting Diana was now at the mercy of her.

"Damn it," I said. "I don't have a choice. Now that they're out I'm the only one who can…"

Something loud fired. It was deafening. I held my ears as I saw a neon blue lighting strike hit Diana.

Thomas struck her with the gun I made. Christine fell from the sky as the lightning strike engulfed the gorgon's body and pulsed wildly. Suddenly the bolt shot higher into the clouds and took Diana with it. She was headed right towards space. Thomas defeated a demon.

I should have been amazed but I was heartbroken. The weapon meant for Samantha helped avenge her. His love for that monster was so strong that it gave him the power to kill a demon. I got on the ground crying as I tugged viciously on the grass. It hurt like nothing I had ever felt before. It was like some deadly acid was burning my insides. How could he love something so terrible?

I watched him walk to Christine as she lied on the ground. She was beaten up pretty bad. I doubt she could have moved. She looked at Thomas and coughed.

She said, "Way to go. You killed your first demon."

"Now I'm going to kill my first angel," he said coldly. I watched in horror as he aimed it at her. He was crying. He said, "Bring her back or I end your life."

Christine said, "I can't bring demons from Hell. I only send them back there. And I'm a sworn protector of the souls in this realm. I wouldn't bring her back even if I could. So go ahead and fire."

He shouted, "Bring her back! I'm not kidding around." He bent down to her and grabbed her.

He shouted, "Samantha isn't a demon! She's human. You have to bring her back. She's somewhere down there alone, scared and hurt!"

I ran to him and grabbed his shoulder. I said, "Thomas. She can't bring demons from Hell. It's forbidden."

He turned to me and gave me the most violent glare I had ever seen. He aimed the gun at me and that's when I couldn't control my crying anymore. I threw up my hands and cried, "You would kill me over her?"

I could tell he wanted to. But it was still Thomas. He was too loving to kill me. He put the gun down and slammed his fists on the ground. He screamed over and over again. I tried to comfort him but he kept pushing me away. I might as well have been dead to him. He wasn't even looking me in the eye.

I saw Christine looking at the sky. At first I thought it was just the clouds or maybe the horizon. But her eyes were following something and she looked terrified. I looked back and couldn't believe it. Diana was falling from the sky. Somehow she avoided being fired into space.

Christine said, "Caroline. I can't fight her like this."

I said, "Thomas. Give me the hell-fighter. Hurry!"

He stood up and turned to Diana. He took one slow step after another. He was like some lifeless corpse. He aimed the gun at Diana. I got in front of him and stopped him.

"Stop," I said. "You got lucky last time! She was distracted. But now? No way. She's way too fast."

He laughed. "So are you. How'd you get in front of me so fast? Best friends for 18 years yet I don't even know the real you. You hypocrite. You even know about heavenly weapons."

I grabbed him by the collar and said, "You don't know what I am because of things like this! I didn't want to draw demons and monsters to you like she did. I'm protecting you. For 18 years you never got into any danger. Ask me why!"

He said, "Let me guess. You?"

"Exactly. Me! So stop treating me like this, give me the gun and go to Christine. Now!"

He laughed and pushed me aside. He said, "I never asked for you to protect me. Stay out of my life, Caroline."

He was hurting me and pissing me off at the same time. I looked back and saw Diana standing in front of us. The entire left side of her torso was badly burned. As she walked, her arm started to crumble away into ash.

272

She spat up blood and roared, "You, mortal boy! Look what you've done to me. I'll eat you alive!"

As she ran at us Thomas shot another round. But it missed. I pushed him out of the way as Diana clawed at him. I caught her fist. She looked me in the eyes, trying to turn me into stone.

I said, "Won't work. My mother taught me how to use my eyes when we found out that leech was here."

Diana laughed. "You've got the wrong idea girl."

She kept looking at me. Then her eyes shifted right. What was she glancing at? That's when I gasped and looked back. Thomas was staring at Diana with his mouth open. I watched his fingers twitch as his body started stiffening and turning grey.

"No," I muttered. "No!"

I ran to him but I was too late. His body was turning to stone. He was slipping away and I couldn't do anything about it. As I screamed and cried for him, lighting strikes lit up in the sky as the ground shook in front of us. I held the statue so it couldn't fall and leave Thomas's stone body in pieces. I could hear the demon laughing. She was coming at me.

She said, "I can't believe a mortal wounded me like this. I'll destroy that statue so there's no hope for his life."

I turned to her and got in front of the statue. Her hair grew into giant man-sized serpents.

The gorgon laughed and said, "Do you wish to fight me little girl?"

"Fight you? No. I want to kill you."

With Thomas dead there was no point in holding back. As the snake heads launched at me, I ran to her. I was too fast for her to see me. Her body flung backwards from the heavy force of my fist to her face.

She landed on her feet and took a few seconds to gain her senses. I stormed her relentlessly with a barrage of kicks and punches. I was too fast for her to react to, but all of my blows were useless. She kept healing after each hit.

She laughed and said, "My eyes don't work on you and you're faster than me. But I can tell you're holding back. Aren't you?" She looked at me and smiled.

I jumped backwards a few yards and landed. She was right. My true power wouldn't surface unless I showed my true form. I couldn't defeat the demon without transforming.

But what was stopping me? I looked back at the statue and saw Thomas watching me. Although he was dead, I could feel his eyes upon me. Waiting. Longing for me to show my true self.

She said, "Careful! If you don't pay attention you

might lose a limb!"

I heard her laughing and looked to see her snakeheads lunging at me. There was no time to dodge. I jumped at the snakes as they coiled around me. As I shot through them they dropped to the ground tossing and hissing. The demon grinned at my claws that had come from my hands.

She said, "Why are you so hesitant to transform? Come on. Are you afraid the statue will see?"

I said, "Shut-up!"

She said, "Poor girl. You're ashamed. Why bother with a human huh? They could never understand a monster. Wait. That's Samantha's lover isn't it? So who are you?" She started giggling and taunting me. I took the bait.

I stomped the ground and said, "I said shut-up! Or I'll rip your throat out!"

She said, "Then do it. Come on. Show me."

I looked back at the statue. Thomas. I was terrified. I knew he was dead but I still couldn't bring myself to show my true form with him there. I turned to the demon as I tried my best not to sob.

But the tears had already started flowing. As I lifted my wrist to wipe my face, I felt a sharp pain in my leg. One of the snakes I cut from the gorgon's hair had bitten me. I started stomping them all in a tearful rage as they swarmed my feet.

The gorgon clapped and cheered.

She said, "Good girl! Show us that monster. Transform for us."

I managed to kill the snakes but my body started going numb from the poison. I staggered back and fell on my knees. I finally gave up and started crying. Why couldn't I transform and save him? It killed me to think about how Samantha Black would have handled things. No doubt about it, she would've killed the gorgon as fast as possible. Even if it meant showing Thomas what she really was.

She would have shined that hideous smirk with those ugly fangs and sickening red eyes. How was she so brave? How did she have the guts to show him her true form? What killed me the most was she still won his heart. I could just see her there in my mind giving me that stare. No emotion. Yet I could hear her thoughts so clearly. She thought she was above me. From day one that was how she always looked at me.

I shouted, "Damn you, Samantha Black! Why did you have to show up? I hate you so much!" I punched the ground.

The gorgon walked in front of me.

She said, "Looks like Samantha ruined both of our lives huh? I know the feeling!"

She kicked me hard across the face. I fell over as she started kicking me again and again.

She said, "Which is why I should have been the

one to kill her! Hell is too good for her. I wanted her soul! She ruined my life!'

She started stomping on my body. I curled into a ball trying to protect my head and chest. I was too sad and afraid to transform. It was over. She gave me one final kick. I rolled onto my back and coughed up blood. I lied there trying to catch my breath. The demon stepped on my chest and stomped me one last time.

She held her head down and dropped her shoulders. Tears fell from her face and onto mine.

She whimpered, "I feel...empty. I can kill thousands of people. I can eat Samantha's soul. But so what? Lucas is dead. Nothing I do will ever put his cold body back into my arms."

She kept her foot on me as she sulked.

Suddenly a bolt of red lightning hit the ground. A Hell gate opened out of nowhere. I heard the desperate souls cry from Hell as someone walked through the portal. Samantha Black. I couldn't believe my eyes. I watched her grin her ugly smirk. She had returned.

Back from Hell. Was it love? It made my blood fume. I watched her as she held her hands out and tilted her head back. She took in a deep breath and let out the creepiest laugh I had ever heard. Somehow she looked different. Her body and eyes were glowing red as her hair floated with the harsh winds.

She looked to the sky and let out a monstrous scream. Her dark energy gave off frightening vibrations. Everything around us shook as if it feared Samantha's presence. The gorgon finally snapped out of it and looked to see what was happening.

Before I knew it Samantha vanished and appeared in front of her. She grabbed the demon by the face and tossed her a few yards away. Then she looked at me. Her eyes were completely filled with red as she grinned. She didn't even look like herself.

I had never been so afraid. I carefully started backing away as I said, "Samantha?"

She took a single step towards me and raised her hand. But the screech of the gorgon distracted her. It was running at her. Samantha completely vanished. It was too fast for high-speed. It was more like teleporting. She appeared right in front of the gorgon and grabbed her by the throat. She slammed her hard into the ground.

Samantha showed no mercy at all. She started viciously stomping on the gorgon's face savagely as she laughed crazily. With each stomp, the earth around us shook. I didn't know whether to run or stay. I couldn't just leave the statue with her rampaging. But I also didn't know if I was her next target. She was too fast to run away from.

Her voice was so dark and full of rage.

She cried, "Save…protect!"

She stopped stomping on the demon but kept her foot on her mangled chest. Slowly the gorgon started regenerating as she reached for her. Samantha opened her mouth and let out another scream. This time a red inferno spewed from her lungs. Hellfire. It gave off the intense heat of a volcano and smelled like death. When the flames were gone so was the demon. Nothing was left.

Samantha let out another angry cry. When she stopped she started looking around. I couldn't figure out why. She kept saying, "Protect. Save. Protect. Save." It was like she was possessed. I whispered her name almost barely. She turned to me and saw the statue. She stopped grinning and paused for a few seconds. Then she vanished and appeared in front of it. Her speed was impossible. Was she…teleporting?

She slowly said, "Thomas…" Her hair stopped floating as her red glow died out. She put her hand on the statue's cheek and said, "Protect…Thomas." Her eyes flashed red and suddenly lost their glow. She slowly fell backwards and hit the ground. I ran to her and held her in my arms.

I said, "Not you too. Come on! Samantha!" I shook her and to my enjoyment slapped her.

She opened her eyes and held her face. "Ouch!

Who the...Caroline?" She sat up and got in my face. She said, "You? I'll...hey wait. Are you crying?"

I sniffled. "I don't know what just happened to you. But you must not remember. Samantha look behind you."

She looked and saw the statue. She slowly got up saying, "What? No. Oh no. Please!" She ran to it screaming his name. Thomas was a stone statue. Somehow I felt responsible. I couldn't stop crying.

She kept shouting for him. I had to cover my ears. Not to mute her but mute the pain. Mute the reality that the love of my life was gone.

"Shut-up, shut-up, shut-up!" I cried.

She ignored me. She held the statue still calling for him. I got up and grabbed her.

I said, "You'll break it and ruin any chance we have at reviving him! Stop!"

She turned to me and slapped me hard across the face. I felt my neck crack a bit as I stumbled. She grabbed me by the shirt and jerked me towards her.

She said, "I can hear your thoughts. You led that demon hunter here! If I hadn't gotten sent to Hell I would have been able to prevent this! He's dead and it's your fault!"

I cried, "No! This is your fault you filthy leech! You came here and led a demon to him. I was protecting Thomas from you!"

She tried to hold it back. But she let go and

punched me square in the nose. My body flew back and hit the dirt. I would have fought back but I was too sad.

And part of me felt that I deserved to be punched in the face. The truth was, I could have killed the gorgon in the blink of an eye. But I refused because I didn't want Thomas to see my monster form. I was just as guilty as Samantha.

She stood at the statue. She kept holding it and panicking. She said, "There has to be a way to bring him back right? We can bring him back! We have to."

I stood up saying, "Maybe! I don't know the first thing about dark arts though. Do you?"

Her shoulders dropped as she looked at the ground. She fell to her knees and it sounded like she was crying. But I knew better. Soulless monsters like Samantha Black could never feel emotions.

Especially not love. She punched the ground and screamed so loud that I had to cover my ears again. I held my arms not wanting to cry but the tears fell anyway. Thomas really was gone.

I said, "Stop your fake crying! There has to be a way we can revive him. Do you know anything about dark arts? I'm sure you do since you're a demon. How'd you escape from Hell anyway?"

She had gotten silent. When I spoke to her she didn't even look at me. It's like she couldn't hear.

She kept staring at the statue. She was the splitting image of pitiful. I walked over to her and pushed her shoulder.

"No," I said firmly. "We aren't mourning until we know for sure we can't revive him. Get up!" I was expecting for her to snarl something rude or shoot me that terrible gaze like she always did. But her face was blank. She stared at the statue as if the world had ended. Either she was really good at faking her emotions or this beast actually loved Thomas. It pissed me off.

I grabbed her arm saying, "Get off your ass! He won't come back with us just sitting here. We need to find out how to revive him."

"He's gone," she said softly. "He's gone and…it's because of me." She looked at her claws and said, "What have I done? I killed him. I really am a fiend aren't I?" She dropped her arms and got her blank stare back. She said, "A bloodsucking monster."

I hated Samantha Black more than anything in the world. But it was incredibly hard not to feel sorry for her. She looked so hopeless and miserable. She openly called herself this monster. It was like she really was human. I looked behind us when I heard voices. It wasn't from the Delphiniums. A group of runes dressed in armor had appeared. They were healing the others.

"Executioners," Samantha said without looking. She said, "They came to kill, Diana."

"Kill her?" I said. "You killed her." She looked back at me with her eyebrows risen. I said, "You seriously don't remember? You came through a Hell gate with wild hair and glowing eyes. You massacred Diana and burned her until there was nothing left."

She scoffed and punched the ground. "Three. That's three times I've lost control in front of him. Did I hurt him?"

I shook my head. "No. He was already a statue when you came. The moment you saw the statue you calmed down and fainted. Are you telling me you have a split-personality?"

She said, "It's my curse. Whenever I'm angry it gets stronger. Sometimes I black out. When I wake up everything around me is usually in ruins. When I was in Hell I was somehow strengthened and healed. Since I wasn't dead or meant to be there, I was rejected and sent back to this realm. That's all I remember. For the last time. I'm not a demon. I can hear what you think."

I held my head and said, "Well thanks for invading my brain, weirdo. So how are we bringing him back?"

She stood up saying, "He's gone. I understand now. I am one of the tainted. Everyone I get close to will always get hurt or eventually die. I don't belong amongst the living. It's best that I go back to staying away. Isolation and solitude."

She turned to me and looked miserable. The Executioners came to us. There was a man with long and straight black hair leading them. He had one hand on his back, ready to take out the sword on his back. It was the size of a grown man. He stopped in front of Samantha.

He said, "Good. You're alive. Miss Black, where is Diana?"

Samantha mumbled, "Dead. Dead. He's dead and it's because of me."

He didn't understand. Not until one of the other soldiers called for him. She looked just like him. Besides her silver hair, they could have been twins. She was in front of Thomas's frozen body. She nearly fainted when she saw it.

She shouted, "Captain! Captain get over here!"

When he went to the body he reacted the same way. He said, "By Lady Maria! A mortal has been killed with dark arts. Damn it. We weren't fast enough. We have to find that gorgon and fast!"

Before he took out his sword I ran to him. I explained it all. How the demon slayers and Samantha fought Diana. I hated Samantha so much. But for some reason I chose not to tell them about her connection to Thomas.

I did give her credit for killing Diana. But I gave

no mention of her becoming possessed by her curse and rampaging or returning from Hell. But Samantha did something incredibly stupid.

While I was explaining everything she came to us like she was some zombie. She held her wrist out to the leader of the soldiers and said, "Lance. I need to be taken into complete isolation. Maybe even execution."

I said, "Samantha! What the hell are you doing?"

She said, "I'm too dangerous to live freely. Everyone I come near gets dragged into the Hell I'm in. Including the love of my life. Thomas Rouges."

Lance said, "What are you talking about?"

I said, "Samantha! Shut-up! You shut your damned mouth right now!"

She ignored me and cried, "That boy was my human lover! Because of me he's dead. It should be me who's dead! Execute me!."

I ran in front of her and punched her as hard as I could in the mouth. She flew back a few feet and didn't bother stopping her fall. She was hopeless. I could see it clearly. Samantha Black had lost hope in everything.

She was nothing but an empty shell. I couldn't stand it. I ran to her and grabbed her. She just lied there as I shouted.

"You're just going to give up now?" I shouted.

I said, "My best friend risked his life for a wimp like you? You get sent to Hell and he fights for you not knowing if you'll come back. We don't know if he's gone for good! Yet you're giving up? You coward!"

I punched her across the face again and again. She never fought back. Tears fell one after another as I tried beating some sense into her. I don't know what it was. Anger. Sorrow. Regret?

Maybe I was upset for hiding myself from him. Maybe I felt that Thomas would have still been alive if I hadn't broken up with him. I left his fate in the hands of a monster who was willing to give up on him so easily. It sickened me.

As I punched at Samantha, the soldiers stormed me and pulled me off. I watched Lance raise Samantha from the ground and bind her hands with chains. They were going to take her away. Something inside of me ached at the thought of her being gone. Why? I quickly broke away from the soldiers and ran for her.

I pushed Lance away and freed her.

I shouted, "Come on! We can outrun them. I'll get the statue and we'll run away. We can bring Thomas back!"

She said, "Can't you see I don't belong here? Can't you see the sins I've committed?"

I cried, "So now it's time for your atonement!

You can't just give up! His love for you is as big as a damned sun! I saw it with my own eyes."

Lance raced at us. He didn't know what I was. So it was easy to catch him off guard. I vanished and kneed him in the stomach. He gasped frantically for air as he dropped to his knees. Immediately the other four soldiers came at us.

Samantha shouted, "Are you insane? Caroline enough!" I was easily outmatched. When I vanished they vanished and stopped my running path. The girl that looked like Lance knocked me back with her bare hand. It was a warning blow. But I quickly recovered and got in front of Samantha.

I said, "Either help or let's get out of here!"

She shouted at me. "You hate me! Why are you doing this? Let them take me! Can't you see the Hell I'm in? Why are you fighting for me?"

I said, "Because you're all I have left of him. As dumb as it sounds and as much as it sickens me to say it. He loved you. He can't protect you so I will. So help me fight these guys, leech."

I looked at her and finally. Finally I saw her smirk that ugly smirk I hated so much. She got behind me and prepared to help me fight the soldiers. I turned my back to her. All of the sudden my senses blurred and I got dizzy as I started falling. Before I blacked out she softly apologized.

16. *Farewell, Angel*

Humans are so odd. I was sure she wasn't exactly human after seeing what she could do. Even so. Caroline obviously had emotions similar to that of a human. For 200 years I walked the Earth sad and alone.

Every living person I came across feared or attacked me. It made me grow hateful and bitter towards them. Then he made me remember. Thomas reminded me what love felt like. But in remembering that feeling I also forgot the one major difference between them and I. I was no longer human.

I watched Caroline lie on the ground unconscious because of me. There was no other way of getting through to her. She was willing to fight those killers for my sake. No more blood. I wanted absolutely no more blood on my hands.

It became so obvious to me once I saw Thomas's stone body. I was a constant danger to every living person I came in contact with. I had no business walking amongst the living. I wasn't going to let Caroline die for me. So I knocked her out.

"Sorry," I said. "It was a noble thing to do, Caroline. But I need to go away. I don't belong here.

Take really good care of that statue. I do want to bring him back. But even if we did manage that, do you think he'd be safe around me? No. This is the best choice. Goodbye, Caroline."

I wasn't sure if she heard me with being knocked out. Thomas was a statue. The Delphiniums were all on the ground fatally wounded. No matter where I went destruction always followed. So I had to spare everyone and go far away. I watched as Lance and his soldiers came my way.

He shouted, "Don't move! By Lady Maria if you move I will obliterate your body."

I held out my wrist and said, "I don't plan to fight you. Do what you must. Please."

He grabbed my wrists and chained them. He almost took Caroline as well. But I begged him to spare her. As he started leading me away I just watched Thomas. It felt like he was still there. He was watching me and calling for me. I wanted to cry.

"Wait," I said. "Wait! I need to see him once more!"

I ran to him without thinking. It was only luck that prevented Lance from destroying my body. They just watched as I ran to Thomas. I screamed for him to come back to life. I begged him to wake up and convince me to fight them all so I could be with him. I didn't want isolation. I didn't want to die. I wanted him. Him and nothing else.

I cried tearlessly, "Please! Wake up and bring me to life again. Save me from this Hell! You're my salvation. Without you I truly am damned! I have no one else! You're my angel in the darkness. My beacon of light. Make the world pretty again and come back to me…please…"

Slowly I got to my knees and started crying tearlessly. Why did I feel so human with him? Even when my heart didn't pump blood I felt so strongly for him. My body was dead but he brought my soul to life. And in return I couldn't offer him anything. Not even tears. I destroyed him. The darkness inside of me destroyed the only light I had seen in 200 years.

Eventually Lance and his soldiers got tired of waiting. After they healed the Delphiniums they were ready to take me back to Nightingale. Christine was surprisingly not happy to see me being dragged off to either be executed or placed in solitude. She ran to Lance and stopped him.

She said, "Before you take her I need to ask her something!" I could see the frustration in her face. She said, "I've casted away literally hundreds of demons. How did you escape Hell? Tell me! I need to know how you did it!"

Lance and his soldiers laughed loudly. He said, "Poor rookie. She's clueless."

Christine said, "What's funny? Stop that! I need answers! I practice nonstop every day. My techniques are foolproof. Tell me how this ordinary vampire escaped Hell! It's impossible!"

I sighed. "You're a talented demon hunter, Christine. I didn't escape Hell. I was rejected and sent back to this realm. I've told you this over and over. I'm not a demon."

"You mean you weren't lying," she said softly.

Lance laughed and said, "Samantha Black a demon?" He laughed harder. "She's a human with a curse. For the most part she keeps to herself. They probably won't believe she got involved with a mortal. It's a shame because I'd hate to see a sweet girl like her locked away."

She said, "Samantha's innocent? But that can't be..."

They ignored her as they kept laughing. She kept watching me as they started taking me away. It probably wouldn't have made a difference. But I really wished that I could read her mind at that point. She found out the girl she had been stalking actually was innocent. She kept gawking me with a look of guilt.

I said, "Make it up by bringing him back to life, spirit child. By the time you manage that it'll be impossible for him to find me. Farewell."

The Summer Before...

That summer had been the worst one I had ever experienced. My life changed forever. For eighteen years I thought I had gotten lucky. No claws. No silver devil eyes. No fire breath or wings spontaneously bursting from my back because I lost control of my emotions. I could live amongst the humans as if I were one of them. I could spend the rest of my life with him. But my story isn't a fairytale.

I was just a late bloomer. That year before summer the monster gene started waking up inside me. First it was small things like my skin becoming more durable than normal. On the soccer field I always felt pain when the girls kicked me and ran into me for the ball. Slowly I stopped feeling pain from the average human. I hadn't thought much about it until I noticed my speed and strength slowly climbing far above human level.

I kept it a secret. Those things seemed so mild compared to my deepest fear. My sisters could transform so easily. The black wings and skin, silver or yellow devil eyes and the tails that sprouted from their tail bones terrified me. But I was still closer to human than they were. I could control my strength and speed. I could pretend to feel pain.

But the gene kept maturing. Every time I was around him the monster inside of me grew faster. I didn't understand it. He made me feel so happy and loved. How could such beautiful emotions cause something so dreadful?

One day we kissed and my nose got this strong and burning itch. I turned away to sneeze into a Kleenex. When I looked at it there was nothing but ashes. I breathed fire for the first time. It was a tiny spark, so Thomas didn't see it. But it was the closest he ever got. That day, my heart sank at the realization.

My monster gene was dominant and maturing fast. It was a monster growth spurt. It was my first and last. Some came little by little but mine came all at once. I will never forget the painful night.

I had distanced myself from him, fearing that I would spontaneously transform right before his eyes. I didn't know how to control my powers. He didn't understand just like he wasn't supposed to. I didn't dare tell him. Even though it broke my heart every time I brushed him off or walked away from him. I cried every time. That was my transformation's trigger: intense sorrow.

I stayed awake some nights crying myself to sleep. The claws would dig from my fingertips and my feet would grow into large claw liked feet. For a while I was able to keep it secret.

But then I got the eyes. I woke up one night from a nightmare. It was a depressing one. Somehow I had killed him. I woke up out of my nightmare fully transformed. I screamed and roared in agonizing sorrow. That's when my family came in. My sisters were all excited and happy for me but my mother understood my pain.

I never wanted to be a monster.

But I didn't have a choice. She and the twins helped me learn how to control my powers. I had to go away that summer to the ritual grounds for our kind. When I came back I knew I had to end things with him. It was the worst day of my life.

We were by a lake in some grassy field by my home. When he arrived my heart fluttered. I could feel the fiery sensation in my chest. One wrong move and I could have spat up fire. Thomas was a trigger. Somehow my love for him made my monster side more prominent. It hurt because it meant I couldn't be with him.

He walked to me smiling his beautiful white smile as always. It made me feel so warm and comfortable. I had been away from him so long. I had missed him. I had to keep myself from smiling and try my best to be as brutal as possible. It wasn't a welcome back date.

I said, "Thomas. You're here."

He said, "Of course. You told me to meet you here. I've been dying to see you all summer. How was the trip?"

Terrible. Worst trip of my life. But I couldn't tell him that. Not the truth. I said, "Great." I still hadn't turned to him. I couldn't find the strength to face him. The love of my life was slipping through my horrifying claws.

He said, "Caroline are you alright?"

I said, "Thomas there isn't an easy way to say this. So I'll just say it. We can't be together anymore."

There was this very cold and awkward pause. I know he must have thought he misheard me. But the look on his face spoke shock and fear. I almost took it back. Forget about the gene. Try anyway and hope for the best. But I couldn't risk that. I loved him too much to ever place him in danger.

He said, "Can't be together?"

I finally turned to him. I said it so cold and angrily. "I'm breaking up with you! Don't try to change my mind. It's me and you wouldn't understand it. Now go home!"

He came to me trying to hold me. I pushed away, fighting my emotions because if I gave in, I wouldn't be able to end it.

He said, "You aren't making any sense, Caroline! Talk to me. What's wrong?"

I said, "We're over. Make sense of it because that's as clear as I can get." I started crying. I walked past him fast while hiding my tears. I tried my best to leave the worst impression so he would hate me and not miss me. I didn't want him to hurt. If anger would help avoid breaking his heart, that's what I wanted. I'd rather be hated by him than have him hurt because of me.

I cried. "Just move on, Thomas. I can't be with you. The sight of you sickens me and I can't stand to be near you! Never speak or look at me again!"

I ran away before he could speak. I kept running until I couldn't see him. Then wings broke out of my back and I flew high into the skies. I just rested in the clouds, crying myself to sleep as the heartbreak started swallowing me whole.